AF408999

KALI
ON THE
ROPES

ALI KADEN

KALI ON THE ROPES

Copyright © 2024 by Ali Kaden

All rights reserved. No part of this book may be reproduced or transmitted in any form or by any means, electronic or mechanical, including photocopying, recording, or by any information storage and retrieval system, without the written permission of the publisher, except in the case of brief quotations embodied in critical reviews and certain other noncommercial uses permitted by copyright law.

Published by Ali Kaden Books

First Edition

Library of Congress Cataloging-in-Publication Data:

Kaden, Ali.

Kali on the Ropes / by Ali Kaden.

p. cm.

ISBN: 9798785495739

Printed in the United States of America

Cover design by Stuart Bache

Edited by George Verongos

VISIT WWW.ALIKADENBOOKS.COM FOR MORE BOOKS!

This is a work of fiction. Names, characters, places, and incidents either are the product of the author's imagination or are used fictitiously, and any resemblance to actual persons, living or dead, businesses, companies, events, or locales is entirely coincidental.

CONTENTS

1.

News item from New York Times (US.) Daily Edition, September 4, 2022:

SAINT TERESA OF CALCUTTA: 25th Anniversary of Passing Highlights Her Enduring Legacy.

On Monday, the Catholic Church commemorated the 25th anniversary of Saint Teresa, the iconic founder of the Missionaries of Charity.

In a major online poll, she was recognized as the most admired figure of the 20th century for her devotion to God and kindness to the world.

ARYA PICKED UP the newspaper resting in the vacant seat next to her on the subway and read the feature story on her ride from Jackson Heights to Astoria. It discussed Mother Teresa's impactful work in Kolkata, spending decades in service to the poorest of the poor. The life the article presented was hard for Arya to fathom, as she had never ventured far from home or walked the streets of an impoverished third world city. Her father had been born in Kolkata, and it bothered her that she knew very little about the city…and about him.

The train screeched to a halt at her stop. Arya threw away the newspaper and hopped off. A chilly spring night in Queens gave way to drizzle. She walked steadily for ten minutes before arriving outside a dimly lit underground parking garage. This descent that used to fill her with excitement now evoked quiet humiliation. At the lowest level, where only a few cars were parked, a crowd of people gathered under stark fluorescent lights, casting shadows on the cement wall.

When Arya advanced, there was an unsettling shift in the atmosphere. The men's gazes lingered too long, their eyes tracing the outline of her figure with an unspoken brazenness. At twenty-four, Arya's mixed heritage graced her with striking features, a blend of Indian and Caucasian influence, accompanied by long, dark hair and large, almond-shaped eyes.

"Didn't think you'd show up," the bookie said, with fistfuls of money in his hand.

"Did she come?" Arya asked.

"She's here—" he muttered, narrowing his eyes at her through thick-lensed glasses. Having witnessed Arya's decline over the past two years, he was hesitant to put her in a fight.

"She's gonna knock you out."

The desperate look in her eyes told him she wouldn't be changing her mind. He scowled at her, trying to convey his disapproval, before he began gathering wagers.

"Alright fellas, first fight of the night is between two ladies, Chantelle and Arya," he announced with false enthusiasm.

Emerging from the crowd, Arya's opponent stepped into the circle with broad, muscular shoulders and was noticeably taller. Her hair was pulled back into two thick braids. Arya tossed her hoodie onto the trunk of a scuffed-up sedan, revealing her white boxing jersey underneath. She rotated her arms, warming up her shoulders to prepare for the fight.

The bookie made his way through the crowd, collecting cash, repeating names and amounts to the wiry young man following him with pen and pad. When all the bets were made, they tallied the odds at the bottom of the paper.

Arya stepped into the circle opposite Chantelle, and the men formed a wide circle around them.

"Even bet. Double or nothing," the bookie announced.

Arya and Chantelle raised their fists, and the men howled and cheered. Bare-knuckle boxing had the potential to become a savage display, and this crowd wanted blood.

"Fight!"

Shouting enveloped them as they began moving around, circling and feinting. Chantelle fired the first jab, grazing Arya's cheek. Arya countered with a right hand down the middle, knocking Chantelle's head back, drawing a bit of blood from her bottom lip. Personifying arrogance, Arya leaned in to mock Chantelle by offering a clear shot. Chantelle lunged with a heavy right. Arya dodged and retaliated with a flurry of punches. As

Chantelle staggered backward. The crowd held their hands out to keep her from falling, pushing her back into the circle.

Chantelle's next offensive was more thoughtful, and she approached at an angle with her guard up, foregoing hitting the face for body shots. Arya absorbed the punches with a grimace and then sent another hard right into Chantelle's face. She staggered, but remained in the center of the circle, throwing shots back.

Arya was surprised by the resilience of Chantelle's chin, and her strength and endurance became more obvious as the fight went on. As she grew more tired, Chantelle seemed to pick up speed and power in her punches. Arya moved away to put some distance between them, jabbing with her left, but she stayed on her, swinging for a knockout. It was a sweeping right that crashed into Arya's cheekbone. She hit the cold cement face-down with a thud, gasping for air.

"We have a winner," the bookie said, stepping over Arya to raise Chantelle's hand in victory.

Chatter erupted within the crowd. The ones who'd bet on Arya cursed openly at her now as she lifted herself off the ground. Holding his thin arm out for her, the bookie's assistant waited until she found her balance. Steady on her feet, she stepped away from the circle to retrieve her hoodie. Arya slipped it on and used her sleeve to wipe the blood from the corner of her mouth. She stared back at the crowd with glassy eyes, a blurry mass of figures and dim lighting. Her eyes regained their focus just in time to see Chantelle take her payout from the bookie and leave the parking garage.

With the only women's bout out of the way, the next two fighters took off their shirts and stepped into the circle for the next match. Many in the crowd already had their cash wagers in hand, clutching them in anticipation. Noticing Arya's dejected expression, the bookie went over to her as she started up the ramp.

"You're too pretty to have your face busted up like that," he said, catching up.

She turned around, expecting more unwanted comments, but instead, he pressed a thin stack of bills into her hand.

"Find something else to do," he said with a hint of empathy.

Arya didn't know whether to thank him or punch him in the face. She offered a slight nod, put the money in her pocket, and walked out to the street above.

A chill ran through her body as she stepped into the cooler air, and she was already beginning to feel the pain of opiate withdrawal. She pulled on her hood and set out to search for some relief. A couple of blocks away, two men stood under the awning of a convenience store selling bags of heroin. She traded fifty dollars for five glassine envelopes—the transaction took less than a minute—then she walked toward her mother's house. It was conveniently much closer than her apartment, and she wasn't in a condition to wait.

It was past ten when Arya arrived outside the second-floor apartment her father had purchased nearly thirty years ago. Looking up, she could see the living room lights were on behind the drawn shades. Arya entered the lobby and went up the narrow stairs of the two-story brownstone. She used her key to unlock the door and was greeted by the worn-out furniture, stained wall-to-wall carpet, and dated appliances she knew as a child.

Across from the living room, Arya noticed that her mother's bedroom door was slightly ajar. Quietly, she tiptoed toward the guest bathroom and locked the door behind her. Her hands shook as she sprinkled heroin from a glassine envelope onto the edge of the sink. She used a rolled-up twenty-dollar bill to sniff the powder and waited for the warmth and comfort to set in.

"You got lucky," she whispered to a bruised reflection, feeling grateful now for the bookie's charity.

Gradually, the aching in her bones dissipated. The agitation beneath her skin eased, supplanted by a feeling of mild euphoria. She stepped out of the bathroom renewed.

Nearby, on the top shelf of a bookcase lined with decades of miscellaneous junk, was a framed picture of her father, Adan. She picked it up and stared into it, wondering what he'd think if he could see her now. In the photograph, Adan carried her on his shoulders, beaming with pride, his complexion a few shades darker than her own. Losing him when she was seven years old had dramatically altered the trajectory of her life, but she still remembered how caring he'd been. She remembered the nickname he used to call her. "Little Kali," he said. It took her years to learn it was a reference to a Hindu deity he admired. *What would you think of your Little Kali now?*

Putting the photo down, she went into the kitchen and opened the drawer where her mother kept the cash. Arya plucked a few twenty-dollar bills out of the white envelope and shoved them into her jeans pocket. She shut the drawer a bit too hard. Still, Cheri's door remained unmoved.

Now a bit curious and worried about her mother, typically not in bed this early, Arya walked across the living room and peered in through the crack. She found Cheri lying face-down on the bed in a wrinkled dress, sobbing into her pillow.

"Mom? Are you okay?" she said alarmedly, pushing the door open. Cheri slowly lifted her face to look at her daughter, revealing running mascara smeared across her wet cheeks.

"Derek left."

Derek was only the most recent one in the long line of losers. After Adan passed away, Cheri had embarked on a never-ending journey for her next romance. Arya never understood how she willingly made the same mistake over and over again. Arya felt nauseous recalling the countless times her mother had allowed desperation to guide her choices with men. She had been a beauty in her younger years, with fun energy, and an easy name to remember, but those days were gone now, along with her first husband and every single man who came after.

"Did he hit you?" Arya asked, noticing the bruise on her mother's cheek. Similar in size and shape to the one on her own cheek, Arya missed the irony. She stepped closer to examine Cheri's face.

"It's nothing. He didn't… I just—" Cheri stuttered, holding her hand over the mark.

"What?" Arya screamed. "You fell down the stairs?"

"Stop!" Cheri said, "You don't understand."

"Oh, here we go. You're going to talk like a battered woman now?" Arya stood.

Cheri felt her face flush with anger and embarrassment from her daughter's mockery and insults.

"Arya, that's enough!"

"No! I'm sick and tired of having to listen to this bullshit! You can't—"

"Enough." Cheri muttered. "That's enough. I want you to leave."

"You're pathetic!" Arya yelled, as she left the apartment, slamming the door behind her.

2.

IN HER SPARSE studio apartment in Jackson Heights, Arya angrily ripped open two more glassine envelopes and sniffed the heroin off her desk. *I should never have existed,* she said to herself, reeling from another awful interaction with her mother. The walls were bare, but her head was a collage of painful thoughts and memories. For two years, she had managed not to hang one decoration.

Arya often wondered why Adan had picked Cheri. After being raised in Kolkata—Calcutta, as it was then known—Adan had come to the US on a work visa as a software engineer. He strayed far from his culture with Cheri, marrying her only a year after landing in New York. Arya assumed they must not have had much in common since Cheri had never traveled or done much in her life. *He just liked her looks,* she told herself. Her own experiences with men confirmed it, where she gave her body, but nothing else.

She glanced across the small room at the mirror on the back of her front door. In it, she could see her mother's features and her father's skin tone. But the person staring back at her did not have a family, or a place in the world.

Arya's memories of her father were few but sweet. He had been a gentle and loving presence, leaving her with recollections of being held and kissed. As she looked back, it was clear that he'd been the better half.

She wished she could go back in time and feel his embrace again. It was the last time someone had truly loved her.

When he passed away, Arya was robbed of the chance to know his culture. Cheri, out of either selfishness or indifference, didn't keep in contact with Adan's relatives. She knew nothing about India to tell her daughter. Consumed by her fear of being alone, Cheri put all of her energy into finding the next husband, and Arya suffered the neglect. It deepened her sense of loss, as if she hadn't lost one parent, but two.

With Cheri's attention constantly diverted, Arya was left to fend for herself at a young age. She pieced together life's lessons from interactions outside the home and countless hours in front of the television. This patchwork foundation led to lackluster performance in academics and difficulties relating to other people. Even now, Arya spent most of her time alone. In high school, she was fortunate to discover boxing. The sport provided the structure she subconsciously desired, where she learned to strengthen and take control of her body and her mind. She competed in the junior leagues at first, then as an amateur when she turned eighteen. Two years later, she turned pro, fighting several times in front of large crowds.

Even establishing a strong record early on, she found the money wasn't there. To keep a roof over her head, Arya resorted to odd jobs—deliveries, bartending, and retail work to make ends meet. At first, she could balance her work with her passion, but Arya had her demons, too. What had started years ago as a way to deal with stress and depression had blossomed into an almost daily drug habit. It had been over fourteen months since Coach Greg had stopped booking official fights for her.

Clinging to some vestiges of her true self, Arya maintained her membership at the boxing gym, fitting in sporadic training sessions. For some quick cash, she entered an underground world presided over by bookies and hardened gamblers. But the foundations of that life were beginning to crumble, too.

A couple of days after her defeat to Chantelle, Arya went in for a light session at the gym she'd been a member of since high school. Walking through the door, she traded fresh air for the smell of sweat and bleach. Chains rattled as fighters pounded the bags, and a group of about twenty athletes stood around the regulation-size ring in the center. The young class, mostly under twenty-one, watched as two young men sparred lightly inside the ropes, practicing footwork and angles.

Coach Greg stood a few feet back from the platform, chatting with a student while his eyes stayed on the ring. At the end of the round, he was surprised to turn around and see Arya working up a sweat on one of the heavy bags.

"We hosted a tournament here yesterday; why didn't you come? And what happened to your face?" How quickly he went from cordial to exacerbated revealed his diminishing patience with her.

"I couldn't make it—" Arya said, continuing to punch the bag without stopping to look.

"I don't want you fighting unless it's a sanctioned bout, you hear me?" He held a hand out, stopping the bag. Arya huffed and put her arms down. "You're going to make yourself useful—you're sparring in ten."

"Okay, Coach."

To diffuse the tension, Arya nodded and went to wait ringside.

When it was time, he came by with headgear for her to use. Arya popped in her mouthguard and climbed up through the ropes. Her sparring partner, a tall blond girl with freckles and blue eyes, entered from the other side. She didn't know her, and the girl looked quite young. Arya expected an easy session but, from the start of the three-minute round, she felt off.

Sensing weakness, the blond fighter pestered her with jabs and feints, messing with Arya's timing. She had fast hands and excellent conditioning, hardly seeming to tire as the round went on. Every so often, she slipped in a hard right hand that pounded against the top part of Arya's headgear. With twenty-five seconds remaining, Arya retreated, outboxed and dizzy.

Coach Gregg called a timeout, and the fighters headed to their corners for a minute's rest. After her loss to Chantelle, the clash with her mother, and now getting bested in the ring, Arya felt her anger rising. In round two, when the girl closed in on her with the long jab, Arya retreated, but with the fierce desire to fight back.

Not just against this girl but against all the things wrong in her life. On the second offensive, Arya slipped and countered with an explosive left uppercut that came up underneath the girl's headgear, connecting with her chin, jerking her head back. She fell onto the canvas, knocked out cold.

"Fuck!" Coach Gregg screamed. "You're just sparring!"

"Sorry, Coach," Arya muttered through her mouthguard, stepping back as he came rushing into the ring.

Arya climbed down and disappeared into the locker room. When she returned, dressed to leave with her duffle over one shoulder, the blonde girl was sitting on one of the benches with her head down, holding an icepack to her lower jaw. Arya looked wearily across the gym floor at Coach Greg coming to yell at her.

"What the hell was that?"

"It was an accident."

"You haven't been right in a long time. You show up, your face all banged up and knock my student out sparring. What the hell am I supposed to think?"

"I didn't mean to hit her that hard," she said, dropping her bag on the ground between them.

"Listen, you can't just—" he stopped mid-sentence as his eyes fell upon her open gym bag. He reached down, picking up a small zip-loc bag that had fallen among clothes and gear. "You think I don't know what this is?" he said.

"Give me that!" Arya said, trying to snatch it away. He raised his hand to keep it out of reach and saw in the light that there was a bit of powder inside the translucent bag.

"You're bringing drugs to my gym? I don't want junkies here. You're a loser. I'm done trying to make you cooperate."

"Coach, come on—"

"Get the hell out!"

"Fine! Fuck you! And fuck your gym!" She snatched up her bag and stormed out.

Fuming, Arya walked down the street eyeing the people passing her, looking for the one to say something out of line. *I dare you to say something,* she beckoned with her gaze. All the years of knowing Coach Gregg, in the end, hadn't made a difference. He kicked her out when she needed him the most.

The bigger problem at hand was there were no drugs left, and without enough cash to buy more, Arya was desperate for a fix. She scrolled through the names on her cell phone and stopped on Richard. An older married man with a second condo overlooking the midtown skyline where he entertained young women and used drugs. On a Friday night, he was her best option to get high without having to resort to more desperate measures.

He picked her up a few hours later in a white Mercedes. Richard didn't buy his drugs from men on corners—he used exclusive delivery services that bought him wide assortments straight to his door. The casually dressed young man who came to the apartment pulled a case out of his designer carry bag that was filled with multicolored pills of every variety. He also had dozens of one-gram vials of cocaine. Richard bought plenty of everything, and whatever Arya wanted, which turned out to be a dozen oxycodone pills in lieu of street heroin. They wasted no time popping pills and cutting up lines of coke on Richard's coffee table.

With the opiates and cocaine in her system, Arya let Richard do what he wanted. In the dim light of the apartment, with his soft gut hanging over the small of her back, dripping sweat, he took his pleasure. The whole affair lasted about twenty minutes, a blur of dissociation and disgust. When it was done, Richard went into the kitchen to bring out the drinks.

Arya heard cabinets slamming shut and glasses clinking against a quartz countertop. She stared at her reflection on the mirrored table in between lines of white powder.

"I hate you," she said, punching herself in the chin.

"What the fuck are you doing?" He walked in with a silver tray, holding a bottle and glasses filled with ice.

"I can still feel."

"Feel what?"

"Everything," she said, before leaning forward to inhale another line.

3.

WITHOUT THE DISCIPLINE boxing brought, Arya lost control, and her drug use escalated rapidly. In late August, months after getting kicked out of her gym, Arya stood on the street, selling her body, something she said she'd never do. With addiction so prominent in her life, this was the only way for Arya to get the cash she needed, the only job she could keep. What used to last her a week only lasted two days, and she lacked the money to sustain her habit. She turned to needles to maximize the effects of each dose, knowing every last bit made a difference in her suffering, and now she lived in constant fear of going into agonizing withdrawals.

Under the harsh glow of a streetlamp, wearing a hooded jacket over a short dress exposing her thighs, she stared into the passing cars. Her eyes reflected the headlights as she waited for the one to stop. A few parking spaces away, in the nearby sedan, her friend Rachel kept watch. Every so often, Arya looked to her because she would need that promised ride to the Bronx if she couldn't hustle up some money soon.

A black SUV turned and pulled up to the curb next to Arya. The passenger window came down, and she leaned over the gap, resting her elbows on the door. She conversed with the driver for a minute. Unexpectedly, instead of slipping into the passenger seat as Rachel anticipated, Arya stepped back, shouting into the window just as it began to ascend. The SUV swiftly pulled out, merging back into the stream of cars.

Nights like this chipped away at whatever remnants of her dignity remained. She looked up to the night sky as an icy drizzle began to fall. She winced as every droplet felt like a tiny prick on her skin. She slowly drew the hood over her face and made her way back to the car.

"Fucking creep," Arya said, slamming the passenger door shut.

"What did he say?"

"I can't even repeat it."

"It's just not a good night," Rachel said, speaking as if it was a set thing.

Rachel had wispy blonde hair and was very thin. Her small stature made her look like a child behind the wheel, which wasn't far off the truth. Arya knew that her running partner had been a drug addict since the age of fourteen, and the tops of her hands and skin of her forearms bore the evidence.

"I'll go see T," Arya said in a defeated tone. "Can you take me?"

"You hate him…" Rachel replied, trying to sound empathetic. She knew what going to him meant.

"I need something tonight. I can't wait."

"Yeah… I only have a little to get me through until tomorrow," Rachel said, subtly excusing herself from sharing.

Arya wouldn't have asked anyway. When it came down to the last fix, addicts knew altruism was out of the question.

"I'll take you there."

Rachel drove her car over the bridge to Manhattan, and then further into the Bronx, exchanging few words on the way.

Terrance lived on a residential street lined with tired three-story brownstones, a few short blocks from the bodegas and laundromats on the avenue. As usual, a group of young men stood outside his building, selling bags, and keeping an eye out for police. Arya stepped out of the car onto a sidewalk littered with broken glass, cigarette butts, and scattered escort flyers. She walked straight for the entrance with her head down, avoiding looking anyone in the eye.

Inside, a narrow stairwell took her to Terrance's third-floor apartment. He cracked the door open a few inches to see who it was before letting her in. His disheveled lanky frame towered over her with matted-down hair, dark circles under his eyes, and pale skin. He wore only a pair of plaid boxer shorts, revealing a collection of faded, amateurish tattoos on his arms and chest.

"Come in," he said with a rasp.

The lights were dim, and grungy music rumbled in the background at low volume. Clothes and papers were strewn everywhere. A bed with a metal frame sat in the corner, pushed up against the wall, with sheets tangled and twisted on top. Beside it hung a poster for the 1977 film "Rocky," which Arya strongly felt Terrance didn't deserve to have on his wall. A guitar with two strings missing leaned against the opposite wall, with the closed case thrown nearby.

Arya put her bag and jacket down on the floor beside the bed, hoping Terrance would give her a shot before he did what he wanted to do. Nothing about Terrance appealed to Arya, except his ability to get good heroin. As a go-between the drug gangs and street teams, he moved multiple bricks of carefully weighed and bagged heroin each week. Barely a player in the game, his only asset was his relationship with the one he called "the Big Man."

"I need something," Arya said, rubbing her hands over her upper arms, feeling a chill ripple through her body and a sniffle under her nose—signs of dope sickness.

"What's the hurry?" Terrance said, creeping up behind her.

He placed his hands on her waist, and she felt his hot breath on her neck. *He's going to make me wait*, she cringed. He slid the straps off her shoulders and pushed her dress down.

"I'm sick," Arya said as she turned to face him naked, trying not to beg.

She hoped he might see the pain in her eyes, but he saw nothing. Having slept with him a handful of times for drugs, Arya knew it would be rough and degrading. Without the numbing effects of the drugs, she closed her eyes and waited for her punishment. Terrance eagerly peeled the rest of her clothes away and took what he wanted.

Afterwards, Arya pulled her underwear back on and sat at the edge of the bed, looking anxiously at Terrance as he rolled over to the other side of the mattress. She fought through nausea to ask for her fix.

"Give me the stuff, T."

"I got you."

He reached into his nightstand and handed her a small plastic bag with a pinch of heroin inside. She at once went to her purse to retrieve her kit and mixed powder with water on her charred spoon. She used a lighter to heat the solution from underneath, bringing it to a slight boil. Then, Arya sucked the solution into her syringe, and traced the crook of her arm with her finger to find a vein. It only took a few seconds, and when she pushed down on the plunger, the discomfort slowly melted away. Arya breathed deeply, and all the tense muscles in her neck and back relaxed.

Terrance watched with amusement from the other side of the bed, then went into his nightstand again to fix a shot for himself.

"You're lucky… I just got the stuff," he said, spilling double what he gave Arya into his spoon. "The Big Man doesn't risk coming by when the block's hot. Even I had to wait."

Arya rested her back against the headboard, letting her body sink into the mattress. She saw Terrence's eyelids flutter as he injected himself beside her.

"I hear that all the time. The block's always hot—"

"Big Man bought his mom a two-million-dollar house. He won't risk what he's got," Terrance said, his voice cracking.

"You going to buy your mom a house, T?"

Arya wouldn't have believed him if he said he would.

"My mom's dead," he said, picking up the remote and clicking the TV on.

Terrance nodded in and out of consciousness, flipping through the channels with his eyes half-closed. Occasionally, he lit cigarettes, but they burned down to the filter, rolling ashes off his knuckles onto the bed.

4.

ARYA STAYED AT Terrance's apartment for a few hours, heavily sedated beside him on the bed, drifting in her thoughts. Terrance greedily fixed another shot for himself, offering nothing to her. He tossed the needle onto his nightstand, lit another cigarette, and went back to flipping through channels. He eventually stopped on one, catching a nod with his eyes closed. It was a documentary about Saint Teresa and her work with the poor in India. In a moment of lucidity, Arya started paying attention.

The documentary showed emaciated families with dirt and sweat on their faces, scavenging through garbage under the hot sun. A quintessentially British voice explained how the remarkable Mother Teresa fought for humanity in a city whose name was synonymous with poverty.

"Much of her work in Kolkata centered around the untouchables, the poorest within the caste system," the narrator explained. "Consigned to begging, sweeping the streets, unclogging sewers, and sifting through rubbish for scraps to eat—they were the ones she believed God called her to serve."

Arya watched with fascination, transported out of Terrance's dirty apartment for a moment to a third-world setting. She wondered if her father had passed by such scenes as a young man. In all the years she'd known he was from Kolkata, she'd never really stopped to think about what it was like there.

"Mother Teresa opened her first hospice for the poor and destitute in 1952," the narrator continued, "in this abandoned Hindu temple in the Kalighat neighborhood of Calcutta."

The footage showed an ornate eastern building, painted white, with a sign outside that said, "Missionaries of Charity. Nirmal Hriday."

"Turn that off…" Terrance mumbled, his eyes closed, the remote resting in his hand.

Arya ignored him. The camera panned the street outside the hospice, and she saw the poor masses, many among them children, in tattered clothes, walking down a street otherwise brimming with life. Merchants sold chai and orange-colored jalebi sweets from their stands, and the kiosks peddled sodas, cigarettes, and snacks. An old man sat on a sidewalk nearby, meditating. He wore only a simple cloth around his waist and a vermillion mark over his third eye.

"I said turn that shit off," Terrance repeated, jerking momentarily, and then nodding off again.

Arya viewed the documentary until the end, learning the remarkable story of the Albanian-born nun who became Saint Teresa. When the credits rolled on screen, she decided it was time to leave.

"T? You alright?" she asked, tapping him on the shoulder as she stood up.

He grunted, a cigarette burning in his hand, but said nothing. She zipped up her jacket and went for the door, stepping past the closed guitar case opposite the bed. Something odd was sticking out from the corner of the case, and Arya bent down to see what it was. She pulled out a crisp hundred-dollar bill. Curious, she gently eased the guitar case open, hardly believing what she saw.

There were multiple stacks of hundred-dollar bills wrapped together, and what looked like a few thousand dollars' worth of heroin, already measured and separated into small baggies for distribution. It was more money and more drugs than Arya had ever seen at one time. She looked over her shoulder at Terrance; eyes still closed, cigarette burned down to the filter. Without thinking twice, she shoved everything into the inside pockets of her jacket and quietly went out the door.

She took a yellow cab back to Queens, and it was only in the dark silence of her apartment did she realize the seriousness of what she'd done. Stealing from Terrance would have consequences, and he'd quickly figure out it was her. Arya placed the money and drugs on her bed and stared in disbelief. She looked through the peephole in her door a few times before attempting to count the money, fearing someone would soon be on the other side. Arya discovered she'd taken just over twenty-five thousand dollars, along with twenty grams of heroin.

After a hot shower, washing all traces of the night off her skin, possessing the two things she spent all her energy trying to obtain each day, Arya wanted to get very high. And though part of her wanted to rejoice, she could not shake the fear that someone was coming to exact revenge. To quiet her mind, she got to work with her syringe and went to oblivion.

In the late morning, fighting through sluggishness, Arya heard her cellphone ringing. A bit of sunlight crept into the apartment through cracks in the shades and she could hear muffled sounds of traffic and construction outside. She blinked her eyes, then looked at the screen. It was Rachel.

"Hey… What's up?" she answered, her voice hoarse.

"Turn on your TV. Channel Four."

"Why?"

"Just do it."

Arya grabbed the remote from her nightstand and powered her television. She flipped through the channels until she found what Rachel had called about. Her face went pale watching the live news report about a fire in the Bronx.

"How late were you there last night?"

"I don't know."

"You don't know what happened?"

"I'll call you back," Arya said, hanging up and turning up the volume.

On camera, a young reporter in a shirt and blazer spoke into a wireless microphone in front of a crowd of people.

"Police have not confirmed the cause of the incident, although early reports suggest the fire started in the third-floor apartment. That resident is the only confirmed fatality so far, but the building is completely burned out. It's still unclear at this time if there are any signs of arson. Our hearts go out to everyone affected on this incredibly tragic day. I'm here with the neighbors, who are now presently displaced."

Passing pedestrians stopped to catch a glimpse and edge their way into the camera shot. The reporter turned to interview a teenage boy and his mother, the first-floor residents.

"Did you know the deceased, the tenant whose apartment is believed to be the origin of the fire?"

"Nah, I didn't know him. Dude always looked high, though," the boy said.

"He was a drug addict," the mother added with a grimace. "Probably fell asleep with a cigarette…and he burns down *our* house!"

Arya clicked off the TV, her pale expression reflected in the dark screen. *Did he pass out and set his sheets on fire?* she asked herself, *Was he overdosed when I left?* It was impossible to know for sure, but she felt a pang of guilt for having been the last one there— especially considering what she'd taken. *But that means no one is coming.* She retrieved the heroin from under the bed, cooked up a shot in her spoon, using much more than her usual dose. Her good fortune was bittersweet because a man was dead, and she hadn't wished it on him.

Sitting with a cup of black coffee in her hand, Arya did some math. She worked out that the drugs would last three weeks. After that, she'd have to start spending Terrance's money to buy more. Once the money ran out, which was inevitable, she'd be back to the usual hustle and degradation. She realized that her current situation was as good as it was ever going to be. Nodding off in the late morning, Arya dared to think about getting clean.

She hid in her apartment for a few days, getting high, entertaining a broad range of emotions following the news of Terrance's death. She felt sorry for his passing, but also relieved to be off the hook. More than anything, she thought about how she could make this opportunity her last goodbye to heroin, and a springboard to getting clean. Before the week was through, Arya had decided that she would finish the last of her drugs and then use Terrance's money to start a new life.

Thoughts of a different type of existence began to percolate in her mind. Arya wished to share them with someone, but there was no one in her life. She couldn't think of a single person to talk to among the drug acquaintances and dealers she knew who would understand. Instinctually, she reached for her mother.

Nearly a week after watching the report on the fire, Arya went to see Cheri on a Sunday morning. She dared tell her the truth, hoping she would invite her to stay and not leave her to go through the torture of withdrawals alone at her weakest and most vulnerable to relapse. Arya arrived at her mother's apartment, looking pale as a ghost and desperate for some compassion.

"Mom, are you here?" she called out, using her key to enter the house for the first time in months.

Across the living room, she saw the bedroom door slowly creak open. Cheri stood there, hair disheveled and falling over her face, having just woken up. There was a man asleep in her bed without a shirt, the sheets pulled up to his waist.

"Shhh! You'll wake him!" she whispered.

"I need to talk to you." Arya gestured for her mother to come into the living room. Reluctantly, Cheri shut the door behind her. She crossed her arms and came forward, a look of annoyance on her face. There was no curiosity in her eyes.

"What is it?"

"I need help…getting clean."

"You're in trouble, and you need my help—"

"I'm not in trouble…"

"I've known for a long time that you're an addict. It's why you haven't done anything with your life. Your choices are not my responsibility."

"Mom, I'm not asking you to take responsibility. I'm just telling you that I'm going to quit, and it's going to be hard, and I need your support…"

"Shhh! You'll wake him!" Cheri whispered.

There's no kindness here, Arya thought to herself as the bedroom door swung open and the man who was sleeping in the bed meandered out with pillow lines on his face, and the bedsheet wrapped around his hairy waist.

"Sorry, my daughter was just leaving," Cheri said.

"I don't want anything from you!" Arya screamed at her, humiliated, rage surging through her body. She took a step toward the man, who was clearly more important to her mother.

"Do you have a fucking problem?" she said, fists clenched, wishing he'd take the bait so she could let out all her frustration and pain

He gazed at them both in confusion, half-naked in the doorway.

"Just get out! Get out, now!" Cheri shouted, shoving Arya to the door.

5.

AFTER ANOTHER WEEK, Arya was down to her last few grams. For the past couple of years, heroin had been her best friend—the only thing that brought her comfort. But it had also brought immeasurable pain and humiliation. Coming closer to the end of this toxic relationship, she knew there would be a void left behind. Boxing is what came to the forefront of her mind. Post-withdrawal, Arya intended to train again and get in fighting shape. Looking at her skinny arms in the bathroom mirror, dotted with injection scars, she made a vow.

"You're going to compete again," she said to the gaunt person staring back at her.

She left the apartment after days in isolation to go to her old gym to tell Coach Greg she wanted to come back. She planned to tell him the truth.

He smiled when he first saw her walking in, and greeted her warmly at the door, but crossed his arms defensively the moment she began telling him about her desire to box again.

"I need to hang on to it…make something out of this, you know?"

"You look awful, Arya. Your skin is gray, your eyes are sunken in… You're high right now—"

"I'm getting clean, trust me. I just need some support…" she said, her voice cracking.

"I can't let you train here again. You closed that door yourself. Go to a hospital."

"I don't have insurance."

"Jesus, Arya."

"If you let me do this, I'll be clean. I won't mess around anymore, I promise."

"I can't trust you to be here. You're a liability for this gym, and for these kids. You know where I stand. I think you should leave."

Arya felt the rejection in her soul and walked away, feeling more defeated than after any fight she'd lost. Discouraged by humanity, she returned to her apartment to sit doubled over on her mattress and get high again.

She spent a few more days hiding at home, until she neared the end of her stash, only a day's worth remaining. Looking at her floor, littered with discarded drug bags, she wondered if she'd be able to resist going to get a fix when the inevitable mental and physical torture began. Her fear mounted over how difficult the undertaking would be and wondered if Coach Greg was justified in doubting her. *Maybe he's right… I'll relapse… I'll never get out of this life.*

The tiny studio apartment started to make her claustrophobic, so Arya went out for some fresh air. She wandered into a nearby park in the late afternoon and found a bench to sit on under a canopy of trees. A young couple sat diagonally across from her, kissing, whispering to each other. She closed her eyes and focused on the soft September breeze that lulled her into a reverie. When she opened her eyes again, the sun had set, and it was night.

At the bench where the couple had been, an Indian family had come to sit. They looked to be taking a short break on the way to some family event. The father sat on the bench, bouncing his daughter on his knee, and the wife sat beside him, sipping water from a bottle. Playing with his daughter, the father spontaneously lifted her overhead, and she giggled in joy. The name, "Little Kali" echoed in her mind. The sound of a homeless woman pushing her shopping cart through the park promenade jolted her back to reality. The cart rattled as the bag lady with frizzy gray hair went from bin to bin, collecting cans, tossing them in her basket. She shot Arya a dirty look as she passed, providing her with the incentive to return home.

At around two in the morning, Arya drew blood as she pushed the plunger down on her syringe, and consumed the last of her heroin. The clock started ticking; she estimated twenty-four hours before her body would start falling apart. She went to sleep easily that night, knowing that would not happen again for some time.

She got out of bed at noon the next day and felt the restlessness starting in her legs. Over the course of the next twelve hours, things got progressively worse. Then the suffering began.

Arya sat at the edge of her bed, compulsively tapping her feet on the ground, cursing at herself and the situation. Her heart raced and her body alternated between fever and chills. Everything from her skin to her bones ached. *It only feels like death*, she told herself, gripping the sheets tightly. Unable to get comfortable, she paced the apartment with nervous energy. When the movement made her dizzy and nauseous, she returned to her bed, collapsing onto the damp sheets, shaking, sweating, writhing in discomfort.

The urge to vomit overcame her in an instant and she leaped into the bathroom, crashing her knees onto the hard tile, and gripping the toilet rim with both arms. She purged everything from her stomach down to the lining, saturating her senses and nasal cavity with the rancid smell of bile. It set her throat and esophagus on fire.

Laying back down, Arya moaned in despair as the walls closed in around the bed, compounding her sense of impending doom. Her thoughts turned against her as she stared at the plethora of discarded drug bags on her floor, thinking perhaps one still had a bit of powder in it to ease her pain. She reached for them one by one and anxiously held them to the light before throwing them back to the ground in frustration. Then she remembered the money under her bed.

She thought about which stoop to visit, or which dealer to call, nearly ready to give up. The clock read six thirty in the morning. It was too early, and there'd be no one on the street selling right now. *Hang on. Stay strong. You can do this*, she tried to convince herself, wrapping herself in a blanket and hugging her knees in the fetal position. Her mind raced with awful thoughts, dissecting her loneliness and shame.

So many nights she wished she could erase from memory—from ever having happened. Arya craved sleep, but the mental torture continued. Memories of standing on street corners and sleeping with strangers pervaded. Her emotions surged. After writhing in bed for hours, battling her body and her brain, she finally passed out a few hours after sunrise.

Her rest was short, hardly restorative, but it was enough of a reprieve from the discomfort to bear a second day of withdrawal. She woke up in the late afternoon still quite sick, though some of the emotional terror had subsided. She took a steaming shower to lessen the cold aching inside her bones. Her thoughts wandered to the money under her bed again, of buying more drugs, but she refused to give in.

Arya had little appetite and could hardly keep anything down for the following three days. She only ventured out of her apartment for a pack of cigarettes and alternated her time between smoking out the window and taking hot showers. She kept the television on to distract herself from the restlessness under her skin and it helped marginally to pass the time.

Slowly, things improved. Making it through the hardest part of the withdrawal—the physical component—Arya prepared herself for the next phase, where she would spend weeks feeling edgy, obsessing over getting high.

With twenty-five thousand dollars in her apartment, staying clean seemed an impossible order. She thought about how easy it would be to get high, without having to do the things she had to do before. *One last time*, she said to herself, entertaining strange fantasies she knew were all dead ends.

Feeling cooped up and crazy in her studio apartment, she looked up a twelve-step meeting to go to. She'd attended one in the past, and it hadn't sat well with her. Trying to keep an open mind, she found one a few blocks from her place, and sat down to listen to a middle-aged man named Paul share his story.

"I'm an addict," he said at the start, leaning forward in his seat. "By the grace of my higher power, and all of you, I have four years clean."

He proceeded to tell his story, focusing on his drug and alcohol use up until the day he stopped. The attendees nodded their heads as he spoke, resonating with the shared experience. Afterwards, he opened the meeting for other people to speak.

"How about you, miss?" Paul asked Arya politely, nudging her to share next.

Arya's stomach knotted as she stared at the sea of faces before her. The prospect of speaking in front of the room felt worse than being naked in front of them. So she stood up and walked out without saying a word.

By the time she made it back to her apartment, Arya had already made up her mind to leave New York.

6.

FOR SOMEONE WHO had spent years wishing for a different life, Arya had thought very little about where she would go. The passport she'd gotten a few years ago remained unstamped. Even with enough money to buy a ticket any place she wanted, only one came to mind. She rationalized the idea, telling herself it was because that's where her father grew up, and the evocative documentary at Terrance's apartment. But deep down, she knew it was a whisper of intuition, and wanted to trust it.

With little knowledge of India and zero experience traveling in third-world countries, she prepared to leave New York, but there was one thing she needed to do first. She had taken money from her mother throughout the years to support her addiction, and now it was time to pay it back. With three thousand dollars in an envelope, she took the train to Astoria. In her mother's building lobby, she put the letter containing the money in the mailbox slot. No goodbye. *Now I owe you nothing.*

A few days later, Arya took a taxi to the JFK airport and maneuvered her luggage through the busy terminal with groups of travelers and airport staff bustling around her.

"I'd like a one-way ticket to Kolkata," she said to the woman at the Indian Airways ticket counter.

"When is your preferred date of departure?"

"Today," she said, placing her passport on the counter, along with enough in cash to cover the cost.

Somewhere over the Atlantic Ocean, Arya fell into a deep sleep, her body convulsing, murmuring fragments of disjointed dreams. The passenger beside her, a distinguished-looking Indian woman in a sari, grew concerned, staring at her distressing state and signaled the cabin crew. When Arya was awakened by the chill from her sweat-soaked clothes, she saw that the seat beside her was vacant. The thought of food turned her stomach, so she looked at the vast expanse outside her window for the rest of the flight.

In Delhi, Arya transitioned to her connecting flight to Kolkata, which seemed to stretch out endlessly, heightening her sense of anticipation and impatience. When the plane finally began its descent into the city, the urban sprawl came into view under a haze of dust and humidity. Touching down, Arya was immediately hit with a unique blend of smells; a humid, tropical scent combined with the raw undertones of pollution and raw sewage. Passport and customs checks were painfully slow, officials taking an inordinately long amount of time for every traveler and their documents.

Eager to get outside the crowded terminal, Arya exited into the hot air to see hundreds more people waiting just a few feet from the gate. Most were taxi or rickshaw drivers, screaming their services to the fresh arrivals. Those with a more foreign appearance were aggressively targeted in hopes of higher fares. Behind them, in tattered garments, stood beggars with hands outstretched towards anyone looking in their direction.

One of the taxi drivers, a young man with shiny hair and a narrow waist, stepped in front of Arya, gesturing to take her suitcase.

"Hello, miss. You want taxi?" Already overwhelmed by her surroundings, Arya agreed. He lifted her suitcase and carried it to his car, a whiff of coconut oil trailing behind him.

"Where you go?" he asked once they were both situated in the car.

"Sudder Street," she replied, "in the Central District."

After doing some research online, she had discovered that travelers often chose the area for its cheap hotels and restaurants.

On the way there, Arya was mesmerized by what she saw out her window. The driver played Bollywood music on his stereo for forty-five minutes, traveling through diverse Kolkata neighborhoods, and she watched the chaos of third-world life surging all around her. The poverty was unlike anything she'd ever seen. Some people waded through knee-deep waters in certain areas where the monsoon rains had collected. Dogs and cows strayed across the highways, stopping traffic. Thousands of people diverged around the car as it traveled—rickshaws, bicycles, and pedestrians of all sorts, making their ways through congested streets. The vehicles seemed to move in a constant state of near collision.

When Arya began to spot restaurants and hostels with Western names printed on their signs, like "Boom Masala," and "Dream Café," she knew they were getting close. The driver confirmed it by saying, "Sudder Street," in his thick accent, and driving slowly for Arya to pick her spot.

"Over there," she said, pointing to a hostel with the name, "Joy House."

He pulled up to the entrance and carried her suitcase up to the threshold. Arya paid in dollars, which pleased him greatly. Passing through the door into a reception area, she saw two men seated cross-legged on the ground, a pot of chai between them brewing on a gas burner. A third man with a jolly, round face sat behind a desk, belly protruding under his wifebeater. Behind him was an assortment of room keys, numbered and hanging from individual hooks. He cheerfully waved Arya over.

"Hello, miss. I am Babu. Manager. You want room?" the man behind the desk said, smiling.

It was humid in the lobby. Arya looked around to see if this was the right place for her. She saw that the far side of the lobby connected with a corridor that led to an expansive open-air garden. International travelers sat at plastic tables and chairs in groups, chatting amongst themselves. The main hostel building sat at the other end of the outdoor space.

"Yes, one room, please. How much per night?"

"Private is four hundred rupees for one night. Two thousand for one week," he said, holding up four fingers, and then two.

Arya used her smartphone to do the calculation. Based on the exchange rate, she handed Babu forty dollars.

"For one week."

"I give change—" he replied, taking the money and fumbling in his drawer.

Handing her back rupees, Babu took a key off the wall, came out from behind his desk and walked with Arya through the courtyard to the actual hostel building—three stories of shared and private rooms, an external staircase connecting the floors. She side-glanced the travelers gathered in their loose-fitting shirts and bandanas like hippies. One group had a portable radio on their tabletop, filling the air with the twangy sound of American country songs.

Babu led Arya to the third floor and removed the padlock from the door, which he gave her, along with the key. He brought her suitcase a few feet into her room, then went back downstairs. It was simple and somewhat dirty accommodation. There was a twin bed pushed up against one of the walls, and a plastic waste bucket in the corner. The paint peeled off the walls, and the tile floor had a fine layer of dust over it. In the bathroom, the shower emptied directly onto a cement floor with a drain.

Arya lifted her suitcase onto the bed and went through it to make sure the stacks of money she'd hidden amidst her clothes were still there. She had buried half of Terrance's money in her luggage and carried the other half on her person. Altogether, she had roughly nineteen thousand dollars remaining. It was enough to last awhile, though looking around her dingy room, she wondered if she'd made a big mistake in coming.

After splashing some water on her face and a change of clothes, Arya went back down the stairs in the late afternoon to explore the area around the hostel. She walked straight through the courtyard and lobby to the chaotic street outside. The street smelled like a latrine. Every second was syncopated with the honks and beeps of vehicles. Weaving through a gauntlet of pedestrians walking in all directions and beggars pleading for change, her senses were saturated.

When she returned to the hostel, the sun was setting, and she saw the courtyard had filled with guests. The travelers, men and women of different ages and nationalities, sat in big and small groups, talking with each other, drinking either water, chai, or beer. Two of the groups looked to be from European countries. Another group was clearly American by their accents. Arya found a lone empty chair at the edge of the courtyard.

Guests called for someone named "Chaiwallah," who turned out to be the waiter—a teenage boy, no older than sixteen. He wore a button-down shirt and plastic sandals, delivering orders and bussing tables. Hot and cold drinks were sold at the hostel, but he also brought specific orders from outside to hostel guests like a one-man delivery service. Arya later learned that the name roughly translated as "tea-boy."

"What you want?" he asked, with clumsy waiter etiquette and innocent eyes.

"I'll have a chai. And can you get me cigarettes?"

"What kind?"

"Doesn't matter."

"Okay," Chaiwallah said, nodding his head politely and leaving to get the order.

At that moment, Arya noticed a nun walking into the courtyard. She wore a white sari with three blue stripes at the hems, the same as Mother Teresa. She was in her fifties and of Indian descent, with soulful brown eyes. She scanned the faces there, looking for someone, but stopped when she saw Arya.

"Are you one of the volunteers?" she asked, approaching her.

"Who?" Arya asked, confused as to why the nun had come to speak with her.

"Volunteer," she repeated. "I'm Sister Maria."

"Volunteer for what?"

Seeing that Arya didn't understand what was being said, the nun changed her question.

"I thought you were one of our new volunteers... What brings you to Kolkata, dear?"

"Just to get some peace," she replied.

"You've come to the wrong place for that!" Sister Maria laughed, and Chaiwallah brought over the chai and pack of cigarettes.

"You're welcome to come visit us," Sister Maria said. "We always need volunteers."

"To do what?" Arya asked, lighting a cigarette.

"To help the poor... This is Kolkata, dear. Many of them are volunteers," she said, pointing at the travelers seated around the courtyard.

Watching her leave, Arya remembered the documentary. It seemed surreal that she was now in that place. Arya considered she might want to volunteer to stay busy, though she had no idea what it entailed.

Heading up to her room, she glimpsed the outside from the top of the stairs. She was shocked to see how many people were sleeping on the street. There were countless bodies sprawled out on single-layer sheets on the hard pavement.

Staring up at the ceiling, waiting for sleep to come to her, Arya was grateful to have a bed that night.

7.

ON AN EARLY autumn Sunday morning, Philip emerged from his hostel room and locked the door. He descended the stairs, ordered a coffee from Chaiwallah, and sipped it in the courtyard before heading out. He walked down Sudder Street to Chowringhee until the ache in his right leg compelled him to hail an autorickshaw to take him the rest of the way to the Saint Teresa's Catholic Church. He arrived almost 20 minutes after the last mass had ended. A large crowd made their way out of the church, including dozens of missionary nuns heading towards the Sister House, their dormitory residence down the street.

The sanctuary was illuminated by the sunlight that beamed through the arched windows. There were a few others there, kneeling in the rows of pews or sitting quietly, practicing their faith. Father Ferdinand and Sister Maria were speaking near the altar when Philip walked in.

"Good to see you, Philip; how are you?" the priest called out, although Sister Maria looked less than pleased to see him.

Philip took a seat in the first row of pews and leaned forward, lowering his head slightly and speaking loudly enough for them to hear.

"I've come to make my confession, Father… It's been two weeks since I last confessed."

"You don't need to confess anything," Father Ferdinand replied with a hint of exasperation. "I've already absolved you…many times…"

"Why come here and waste Father Ferdinand's time?" Sister Maria interjected.

Philip looked up at her sharply, thinking about all the reasons faith no longer mattered. He held back his contempt because it wasn't really meant for them; it was meant for God.

"I'm not wasting his time… I'm wasting mine."

"Find forgiveness through service. Can't you see there is plenty of need around us? You've spent years in selfishness and isolation!" The words came out more harshly than Sister Maria had intended. Philip rose abruptly from the pew, gave her a disdainful look, and went towards the door.

"Will you consider service?" she shouted after him.

"Yes, Sister," he said without turning around. "I'm going to serve myself a drink right when I get back."

He marched out of the church and hailed another autorickshaw all the way back to the hostel.

It was noon when he made it back. Passing through the courtyard, he found Chaiwallah and gave him money to buy whiskey from a black market seller down the street and instructed him to bring it to the roof, along with a glass and some ice. Phillip had hauled up a chair and table from the courtyard. About thirty minutes later,

Chaiwallah appeared on the roof, bearing the imported glass bottle, and the other requested items.

Hours passed, and the sun began its descent as the tension in Philip's shoulders eased. He felt the urge to get up and move. Slipping off his shoes, he stood up and started to throw punches. The emptiness of the rooftop gave him the freedom to shadowbox. It was one of the few things that hadn't changed, so boxing remained a lone anchor to a past that seemed a lifetime ago.

Downstairs, Arya was returning from another neighborhood walk, wandering to pass the time. She walked through the hostel courtyard and headed for her room. When she reached the top of the stairs, she heard a strange but familiar sound coming from the roof. Curious, she went up the last flight of stairs and saw Philip shadowboxing near the edge. It was clear to her from his movements that he had been a real fighter once. He had long scraggly brown and gray hair that fell just under his chin, and by the length of the scruff on his face, he hadn't shaved in weeks.

Philip exhaled sharply with each strike, forcing his breathing into a rhythm. Arya watched, listening to the "esh… esh… esh…" of his shadowboxing until, sensing someone there, Philip stopped abruptly and turned around.

"What do you want?" he asked, a hint of irritation edging his voice. Her gaze drifted to the whiskey bottle on the table and the dirty ashtray.

"Sounded like someone was training." Philip sat down, poured a little more into his glass and lit a cigarette. By his accent, Arya could tell he was English.

"I'm done training," he replied, indicating she might want to move on. Arya stayed, eyeing him curiously. He didn't seem like any of the other guests at the hostel—the volunteers.

"You were a boxer, weren't you?" she asked. Philip finished his glass, then filled it.

"Was. Retired now." Instead of wandering back down the stairs like he'd hoped, Arya stepped closer toward his table.

"I used to spar a bit, back in New York."

"New York, huh? That's home for you?"

"Yeah. And you?"

"Birmingham." He hesitated for a moment before adding, "Whiskey?"

Arya briefly considered taking a drink. Past experiences had taught her that alcohol often led her back to heroin. Merely thinking about it triggered an unsettling craving. Gazing at Philip, with his disheveled hair, outdated t-shirt, and hints of gray in his beard, she didn't get the impression that he was living the life of an athlete. She couldn't help but wonder if he knew where to get drugs.

"You know where to get something...stronger than that?" she whispered, nodding toward the whiskey bottle.

"Like rum?"

"Stronger." She spoke in a low tone and held his gaze. Philip had been around long enough to understand what she was suggesting.

"Do I look like a bloody drug dealer?" he snapped at her.

The words shook Arya back to reality. Suddenly embarrassed, she stormed off down the stairs, and Philip filled his glass with more whiskey and resumed his vigil over Sudder Street.

After nightfall, Philip had Chaiwallah bring him a meal to soak up the alcohol in his stomach. He was determined to break up the monotony of his self-exile with a visit to a fight club he'd heard about, thirty-minutes away by car. On the way there, Philip felt a bit of excitement that comes before any boxing match. The taxi stopped in front of an unassuming one-story concrete building with a corrugated metal roof on a large plot of land in a rundown residential area. Above the entrance was a sign displaying "Balaji Boxing Gym" in bright red letters.

There were over a hundred cars parked outside, signaling to Philip it was a good night to have come. He gave the driver his fare and asked him to wait outside. Mean-looking bouncers dressed in black stood on either side of the door, refusing entry to all the children from the neighborhood and curious pedestrians who were loitering around. Two little girls broke away from the group and stood at a smudged window, attempting to get a peek inside. Philip walked right past them and into the building because expats did not receive the same treatment as locals.

Inside, a large crowd of both locals and expats had gathered around the regulation-size boxing ring in the middle of the hall. Some lounged on the metal folding chairs arranged in multiple rows like an auditorium, while others stood behind them for a better view. There were two cash bar stations serving cold beer and liquor. At one end of the space, heavy bags hung from beam rafters and racks full of exercise equipment showed that this place doubled as a daytime boxing gym.

Philip made his way to the bar and bought a cold bottle of beer before taking a spot standing next to some of the other spectators. The bell rang, and two fighters who looked like middleweights stood up from their corners and moved toward the center of the ring. The taller fighter wore white trunks, the shorter one wore red.

From the start, it was clear to Philip this was an uneven fight. He could see the taller fighter in white had the advantage because the other man lacked the skills to get on the inside. Using his long jab, he opened a cut under his opponent's eye. A referee stood in the ring with them, allowing the fight to happen without too much interruption. Round two ended with the shorter fighter taking a beating in the corner.

Philip bought another beer and moved closer, finding himself behind an elegantly dressed couple. The man wore a navy blazer that belonged in a country club, and his female companion wore a white gold chain around her neck, inlaid with diamonds. They did not look like the type of people who belonged in a dingy boxing gym, but the desire to see violence drew people from all walks of life.

"Who's your money on?" Philip said, striking up a conversation with the couple.

"The taller one, mate," the man said in a similar English accent, turning around to see who he was speaking with.

"Who's offering the action here?"

Ten seconds into the new round, the shorter fighter caught a stunner and landed in the corner, defending against an onslaught of knockout punches. He took a thundering right hook to the temple that chopped him down, and the crowd erupted with cheers.

"Yes!" screamed the Englishman. "Go to Garu's table. Over there, on the other side of the ring."

Philip stared through the ropes to the other side where he saw a middle-aged Indian man in a white suit, seated at his own table, a smug expression on his face and expensive scotch in front of him. Two men who looked like thugs stood nearby, keeping watch.

"That's a miserable-looking guy," Philip said.

"You don't want to get on his bad side. Minimum buy-in is four lakhs tonight."

The referee raised the taller fighter's hand in victory. A ring announcer, wearing a blazer over his kurta and shouting in Bengali into his microphone, gave the details of the next fight. Philip eyed Garu's table, deliberating whether to post a wager tonight or not.

8.

AFTER HER INTERACTION with Philip, Arya could not shake the feeling of wanting to get high. She sulked in her room for the remainder of the day after their interaction, afraid her impulses would drive her to do something reckless. The next morning, hoping for a distraction, she walked the neighborhood, venturing further than before. At a tea stand, she bought chai in a clay cup, drinking it quickly and then, returning the container to the earth, she set off to explore the streets.

Arya walked down Sudder Street and then meandered, arriving in the Central District after fifteen minutes. As she pushed her way through a mass of people, she encountered beggar women asking for money with palms open, using their infants to invoke pity. Arya kept her eyes forward, avoiding direct contact as she saw the locals do. Eventually, she stumbled across Chowringhee Bazaar, an expansive outdoor market where merchants offered an array of items from baskets of spices and local crafts to specialty foods. Arya observed as women pinched produce to test for ripeness, while men weighed mangoes and tomatoes on scales to determine their cost. For over an hour, Arya was immersed in the surrounding life, taken by its divergence from anything familiar to her.

On her walk back, the urge to get high began to take over. She examined the faces passing by her on the street, searching for the one who could lead her to oblivion. Chowringhee Lane was lined with a dozen parked taxis. Arya spotted one of the drivers leaning on the hood of his car. He was thin, wiry, and had an air about him that told her he knew where to get drugs. As she approached him, she noticed his bloodshot eyes and sunken cheeks. He grinned mischievously, revealing tar-stained teeth.

"Hashish?" he questioned in a low voice. Arya sensed she had picked the right person.

"Something stronger…" she responded, her gaze never leaving his red-rimmed eyes.

"Opium?" he said softly, and his grin widened.

"Stronger," she affirmed.

He paused for a few seconds, before offering the next item on the list.

"Brown sugar?" It wasn't a term used in the US, but she knew what it meant. A jolt of anticipation ran through her body, making her knees weak.

"Yes."

The taxi driver waved his arm and shouted to a boy down the street, having a snack at one of the potpourri carts. He rushed over, and the man pushed a few rupees into his hand, instructing him to keep an eye on the taxi until he returned. The boy parked himself by the passenger side door, and the driver invited Arya to walk with him. He led her away from Chowringhee through a narrow alleyway that led deeper into a residential neighborhood. He zigzagged his way through until he arrived at the entrance of a dilapidated three-story apartment building. Arya watched curiously, wondering if this would turn out to be a scam. He went up the three steps leading into the dark lobby and shouted a name.

Suddenly, an old man emerged from the darkness. He was extremely pale and gaunt, with jaundice-yellow skin. His left arm had been amputated mid-bicep—the result of intravenous drug use. The taxi driver conversed with him in Bengali and then uttered the words "brown sugar." The one-armed man pulled something from his pocket, which he showed the driver. It was about a gram of heroin, wrapped in wax paper and folded very carefully to fit into a postage stamp-sized square. The taxi driver gingerly opened it up, revealing its contents to Arya.

As Arya stared at the substance in the crease of the wax paper, she knew that this was what she had asked for. But fear spread through her body and she could not bring herself to take it.

"You want?" the driver asked, holding the folded wax paper out for Arya. The old man glanced at them suspiciously.

"I don't need it—" Arya managed to say, quickly backing away.

"Come on! Take it!" he snapped, his frustration growing as he realized he might have wasted his time.

Arya turned and ran. After navigating the intricate network of residential streets for twelve frantic minutes, she finally saw Chowringhee Road again. Relieved, she followed the familiar route and made it back to her hostel unscathed.

Her room was humid, the ceiling fan whirring noisily, and a column of black ants moved steadily across the floor. She hadn't anticipated how easy it would be to find heroin in Kolkata. *I can't stay here. I have nothing to do and nobody to talk with. Coming here was a mistake.* Pacing between the bed and the door, Arya remembered the nun's invitation to volunteer. She swiftly exited her room, descended the stairs two at a time and dashed across the courtyard, barely registering the faces around her. She approached Babu with urgency, inquiring about where to find Sister Maria.

Babu, sorting through hostel room keys on hooks behind his desk, pointed in the direction of Chowringhee Road.

"You must go to the Sister House," he said, his voice carrying the hint of having directed countless others there before. "You will find her there early in the day."

The following morning, Arya was downstairs, ready to leave at 7:30, and at Babu's suggestion, she hired an autorickshaw to take her to the Sister House. It was a short ride, and she arrived at a massive gray building with brown shutters and a blue sign hanging over the door that read: Missionaries of Charity – Sister House. Inside, a nun directed her to the back courtyard, where Arya noticed other volunteers in loose linen clothing had already gathered under the sun. Beside them stood a group of nuns, dressed in white and blue saris, waiting to give out instructions for the day, sending groups out to various shelters around the city.

"Good morning, everyone," one of the nuns started. "Today, we will have three teams going out." As she spoke, the nuns dispersed, forming pairs.

"For those heading to Karuna Dan, please join us here. Sister Agnes is leading the team to Prema Dan, and Sister Maria to Nirmal Hriday." Each nun lifted a hand, guiding the volunteers. A flurry of activity ensued as individuals made their choices, settling into fairly even groups by number.

Sister Maria noticed Arya standing awkwardly at the edge of the courtyard and walked over to her.

"It's good to see you again."

"Do you still need volunteers?" Arya asked nervously.

"You came at the perfect time. Why don't you come with my group to Nirmal Hriday."

Arya shrugged.

"Home for the dying and destitute… The first that Mother Teresa opened here."

Sister Maria led her group of volunteers out the front gate, headed in a different direction than the other groups.

"What is your name?" Sister Maria asked.

"Arya."

"You're Indian?"

"My father was."

"Do you know the city?"

"Not at all," Arya admitted.

"We're currently on Chowringhee. We'll board the train to Kalighat, then it's a short walk to Nirmal Hriday."

On the subway ride, Arya overheard her fellow volunteers' conversations. They were all from different countries, speaking English with varying accents. Some came on their own, others with non-profits, but they all were there to volunteer with the missionaries.

Upon reaching Kalighat station, Sister Maria led them to an ornate white building that looked like an old Hindu temple from the outside. It was the one Arya had seen in the documentary.

"This is the first home Mother Teresa opened in Kolkata, in 1952," Sister Maria said as she opened the door.

Patient beds filled nearly every square inch of the large open hall. There were 108 in total, with long aisles between them. Nearly all were filled with men, sick and emaciated from disease and old age. Other than the small built-in office near the entrance where the sisters kept files and medical supplies, there were no large fixtures, machines, or screens. At one end of the hall, a partial wall separated the latrine from the common area, but it did little to hold back the smell.

Sister Josephine, a slender nun with light hair and a French accent, brought three of the volunteers upstairs to the kitchen to help prepare lunch for everyone. Sister Maria took a small group over to the basins to show them how to wash bed linens before instructing the last couple of volunteers, two young men from the US, to clean and mop the bathroom. She then came back to stand with Arya near the office.

"What's wrong with them?" Arya asked, looking out over a sea of sick men.

"Most are here because of infection," Sister Maria said. "These are poor people, no medical knowledge or access to supplies. On the streets, with no way to treat infection, it spreads, and they become sick. Our priests go out to find them…sleeping in the streets or on the subway platforms and bring them here."

"It's only men?" Arya asked.

"We have several homes for women as well," Sister Maria replied. "But I work here." She led Arya around the room and stopped at one of the beds.

"His name is Manish. He's been here for one week."

He sat upright in his bed, one leg stretched out in front of him, the other bent at the knee. The outstretched leg had an open wound running from the top of his shin to the back of his calf, clearly infected and full of pus. A Spanish volunteer from the train, who had medical expertise, sat at the foot of a bed. With bandages and peroxide, she carefully drained a mix of red and yellow fluid into a stainless-steel pan.

"She cleans and dresses it three times a day for him," Sister Maria said, continuing to walk down the aisle and then stopping again before a frail old man.

"This is Bishal. He's dying from sepsis," she whispered.

He held his distended stomach in his hands, quietly immersed in his pain. Arya looked down at the dying man with a sorrowful look on her face. Volunteering with the nuns seemed more demanding than she had expected.

"Don't worry, dear, you will be fine," Sister Maria said, reading concern on her face. "Today, help the others with the lunch preparations."

Following her direction, Arya went upstairs and jumped into working side-by-side with the others, cooking for over 100 people. Together, they chopped vegetables and prepared rice, piling it all into giant cauldrons to go over the gas stove. When the food was ready, Arya helped bring pots of curry and rice downstairs to put on rolling carts. She served plates to the men in her section and they ate with their hands, mixing the curry and rice with their fingers. All plates were collected at the end to bring upstairs for cleaning.

After lunch, the volunteers were given a brief respite. A few chose to leave during the break. Drinking chai on the second-floor terrace with her peers, Arya discovered there were two shifts—one in the morning, the other staying through dinner. Despite feeling drained and overwhelmed, Arya selected to stay for the second shift.

Arya found Sister Maria and Sister Josephine on the first floor, scrutinizing medical records to guarantee every individual was given the drugs prescribed by visiting doctors. They then put tablets in small white cups marked with bed numbers before delivering them to each person.

Returning to the kitchen, Arya found herself immediately engrossed in assisting with a new curry recipe. Guided by the nuns and other volunteers, she blended spices, diced vegetables, and stirred the large cauldrons. Then came the second clean up. Staying through to the end of the second shift, she was glad when it was finally time to leave.

"Will we see you here tomorrow?" Sister Maria asked when Arya was about to depart.

"Yes, Sister. I think you will."

When she exited Nirmal Hriday to the street, the sun had already set, but there were still lingering streaks of light in the air. The temperature had dropped a few degrees, making it cool and comfortable atmosphere for her walk back to the train station.

9.

News item from the Darjeeling English Times, Daily Issue, October 19, 2003:

BEATIFIED Saint of Gutters

Hundreds of thousands crowded St. Peter's Square Sunday, celebrating Pope John Paul II's beatification of Mother Teresa, known as the "Saint of the Gutters."

Mother Teresa was awarded the Nobel Peace Prize in 1979.

THE NEWS OF Mother Teresa's beatification was a cause for rejoicing among Christians in India and around the world. One step away from canonization, Mother Teresa—known worldwide for her works with the destitute in Kolkata—would now be called Saint Teresa. Yet the announcement was marked with sadness for Sister Maria, who had been inspired by Mother Teresa all her life, and now stood looking out the window of her classroom.

Outside, clouds swept over towering mountains, parting occasionally to allow sunlight to grace Darjeeling. Nestled in the foothills of the Himalayas, the town offered a breathtaking panorama, with views of snow-capped peaks in the Annapurna range. Everywhere one looked, there were lush tea plantations, rolling hills, and lofty mountains. Darjeeling was not just a visual symphony, but also a sanctuary for those seeking respite from the chaos of city life. It attracted a diverse array of visitors, from locals seeking solace to Tibetans, Nepalis, and a constant stream of European and American travelers.

As Sister Maria admired the view, she felt a deep sense of gratitude and prayed silently. *Thank you, God, for this momentous day. Please grant me the strength to fully appreciate and embrace it.*

Her gaze shifted to the school courtyard below, where students dressed in pristine white shirts and long, flowing blue skirts were beginning to assemble. The students gathered in small groups, chatting amongst themselves, waiting for the bell to ring so they could enter the building.

The beautiful view at the top of the world, and the regal Victorian architecture of Saint Catherine's Academy only reminded Sister Maria how far she was from where she wanted to be.

Sister Maria felt a strong calling to serve the poor, much like Mother Teresa did, and she wanted to join the Missionaries of Charity in Kolkata. It wasn't common for nuns to change their orders, but she had the courage to ask for it. Moving from Darjeeling to Kolkata wasn't a typical request either, but she was willing to make that sacrifice for her faith. Despite her sincerity and devotion, her request to leave her current order was never answered by Revered Mother or anyone else in charge of assignments at Loreto.

God, you have instilled this desire in my heart. Will You grant me the opportunity to fulfill it?

Born into a modest Christian family in Goa, Sister Maria was an unusual child, who displayed an early and uncommon commitment to her faith, expressing a deep desire to dedicate herself to the service of the Lord. At the age of eighteen, she joined the Sisters of Loreto in the former Portuguese capital of Velha and started her vocational training to become a teacher. Following her training, the order assigned her to Saint Mary's High School in Darjeeling, where she taught catechism and geography for seventeen years.

As her young adolescent students streamed into the classroom, Sister Maria shifted her attention away from the window, focusing on the task at hand. Seated at her desk, she waited patiently until every student had taken their seat. Once the classroom was calm, she began her lesson. With a low and shaky voice, she instructed the girls to take out their notepads and pens. From her doctrinal manual, she read a series of catechism questions, prompting the students to answer out loud.

"Who made you?"

"God," they answered.

"What is the penalty for sin?"

"Death."

"How do we recognize true faith?"

"It yields good works."

"Please, take out your notebooks and begin writing the Apostles' Creed," Sister Maria instructed.

During the ensuing silence, her thoughts drifted to the existential suffering of her predicament. She was acutely aware that compassion was welling up in her heart because her soul had a sacrifice to make. She wished to give herself entirely—whatever was left of her life, in service of the poor. Her heart ached for the people she knew went to bed hungry each night, dying cold and alone without the loving hand of mercy to guide them home. In the grand enormity of creation, this sacrifice seemed insignificant in the face of all suffering, yet so profound by how deeply Sister Maria wished to give.

Not all your children are willing to dedicate themselves to you. Not many would leave the comfort of Darjeeling for the chaos and misery of Kolkata. But I am willing. Why do you deny me this?

Sister Maria found it particularly unjust that God would instill such an ardent desire within her heart, only to seemingly withhold the means for her to pursue it. The announcement of Mother Teresa's beatification had exacerbated the ache in her heart, leaving her haunted by the fear of never fulfilling her true purpose. The thought of departing from this world without having embraced the role of a mother, whether to her own children or to those in need, weighed heavily on her mind.

Once her students had completed their notebook entries, Sister Maria commenced her lesson on the virtue of charity—the practice of loving God and all His creations for His sake. However, the words she spoke felt hollow, for beneath her teaching, a simmering resentment tainted her ability to feel love in that moment. Instead, she felt anger and frustration.

For four long years, the thought of changing her religious order had constantly been on Sister Maria's mind. Over eighteen months had passed since she officially submitted her request to the Revered Mother. Endless waiting had been her fate, marked by a lack of assurances and an abundance of reminders to maintain patience and gratitude. Out of sheer frustration, Sister Maria had taken the extraordinary step of sending a direct letter to Father Patrick, the overseer of assignments and transfers for the Loreto order in Darjeeling—a man rumored to possess a direct line to the Vatican.

Six months went by, and still, there was no response. She could remember the words of her letter because she'd written it three times. It was dispatched through regular mail, and there was certainly a chance it could have been lost in transit. However, Sister Maria held an unshakable conviction that her destiny, for reasons unknown, was deliberately being withheld.

As she went around the classroom, handing out the next assignment, she noticed the dark bruise beneath Priya's eye. She'd seen marks on her before, and she suspected she knew where those marks had come from. Among the families who entrusted their daughters to Saint Mary's School, faith was not always the guiding force, and she knew that a man who would harm his own daughter had little.

After the last class of the day, Sister Maria followed Priya down to the front courtyard where her father would be picking her up and approached her gently.

"Priya, can you tell me what happened?"

Priya tentatively touched the bruise under her eye, then glanced away. Tears welled up in her eyes. In the courtyard, students poured out of the building, some walking home with friends, while others waited for their parents or family drivers to arrive.

Among the crowd, Priya's father made his way over. He bore the features of Bengali heritage and was particularly well dressed, his expression marked by an unsettling sternness. Sister Maria could see the fear in Priya's eyes as her father approached, confirming her suspicions about the cause of the bruise.

"Did you hit your daughter?" Sister Maria demanded.

"What are you talking about?" he replied defensively. A shadow of fear passed over the girl's face.

"Your daughter is frightened of you," Sister Maria stated, her voice cold and accusatory.

"That's none of your business," he retorted, anger flashing in his eyes. "I am teaching her to behave!"

"Then I will do the same for you!" Sister Maria said, grabbing him by his shirt collar.

He tried to break free, but Sister Maria would not let go as she pushed him toward the school gate. The commotion caught everyone's attention, with nuns and staff rushing over. As hands reached in to pull them apart, Sister Maria pushed back, her anger clear for all to see. Then she caught sight of Revered Mother's long face.

"Enough, Maria," she said with a firm tone.

Taking a deep breath, Sister Maria let go of Priya's father, releasing him to startled teachers and went back into the building, leaving them to deal with him. She walked straight through to the back and entered the faculty section, headed for her room. Behind the solid door, as she sat on her bed, Sister Maria braced herself for the knock that never came. After a little while, she regained her composure. Biting back her pride, Sister Maria returned to go through the rest of the day.

In the faculty office, as she marked assignments, she could feel the weight of watchful eyes. Supper was no different. She took her usual seat in the dining hall, trying to focus on her meal, but the hushed whispers and side glances from fellow sisters made it difficult. Evening prayer, usually a time of peace, was marred by the same uncomfortable energy.

She returned to her chamber after a long day, finding solace in isolation. Exhausted in body and mind, she gratefully reclined on her bed. Although she welcomed the privacy for now, the dread of a scolding at sunrise lingered in her thoughts. Sister Maria was grateful to put on her single cotton nightgown and let her hair loose.

Only when she was finally alone in her room could she let her emotions out. She looked at the few things she owned, two changes of clothes and books scattered about the room, then at her own reflection in the mirror, and burst into tears. She stood, willing to give every last thing she owned to God for the chance to serve him.

"Why have you abandoned me?" Sister Maria whispered.

These words, she recalled, were the same uttered by Jesus during his most vulnerable moment on the cross. A moment where, even in his divinity, he felt the profound anguish of humanity. Similarly, she felt severed from her purpose, denied the chance to serve God. The day's events were a testament that her yearning to serve, if unfulfilled, could twist into bitterness.

Sister Maria grappled with a yearning that transcended the vows she had taken. Deep within her, a maternal instinct, potent and unfulfilled, stirred restlessly. Though she bore no children of her own, she found solace in the notion of motherhood, cherishing the profound significance it held. In her sadness, she turned to something not of her own faith—Kali, the Hindu embodiment of the Divine Mother.

Despite what many of her colleagues held in prejudice, she understood that in the Hindu tradition, the many manifestations of divinity were but facets of a singular divine essence. Yet, she also knew the gravity of her actions. Christians weren't meant to worship Hindu gods, and it was more egregious for a Catholic nun, for whom excommunication was a real possibility if ever discovered.

Opening one of the books stacked on her desk titled *Places of West Bengal*, Sister Maria thumbed through the pages until she landed on the section about Kolkata. In the first spread of photos, she studied the picture of the Kali statue kept at the Kalighat temple at Dakshineswar and read the caption underneath.

"Kolkata is the city of Kali, named for its deep connections to her, where she has been fervently worshipped for millennia. The city's original name is Kalikshetra, or 'Ground of Kali.' In Hindu tantric traditions, she is a revered and benevolent Mother Goddess, embodying the nurturing and consuming forces of the cycle of life."

The statue was made of black stone, stark against the page's backdrop, her tongue jutting out, and a garland of flowers hung around her neck. Sister Maria traced her fingers over the image. In a sudden surge of emotion, she closed her eyes and chanted to the mother goddess, a mantra she had committed to heart, but never used.

"Om Klim Kalikayei Namaha! Om Klim Kalikayei Namaha! Om Klim Kalikayei Namaha!"

The prayer that Sister Maria offered was an innate call from the depths of her being, for her life to embody the essence of Kali, the enigmatic power of the feminine aspect in its full potency

"Om Klim Kalikayei Namaha! Om Klim Kalikayei Namaha! Om Klim Kalikayei Namaha!"

The mantra had a rhythm of its own, transforming the stillness around her, and the walls seemed to pulse with delight.

As soon as Sister Maria finished saying it, she felt a hint of Christian guilt, though she knew better. Putting the book back in the pile, she slipped off her shoes, flicked the lights off and settled onto her bed. The dimness of her room was broken only by a faint glow from the window. The night breeze stirred the curtains, and she watched them sway, brimming with nervous energy.

It took a while to fall asleep, and when it came, it was not restful because of a very unsettling dream.

She stood in her classroom, but it was night and very different. The desks sat empty, bathed in a moonlit glow. Shadows floated across the chalkboard, and a distant, pulsing drumbeat echoed through the silence, merging with the chant, "Om Klim Kalikayei Namaha! Om Klim Kalikayei Namaha! Om Klim Kalikayei Namaha!"

Out of the corner of her eye, she saw movement. Turning, she faced a towering figure emerging from the corner. Her inky skin seemed to drink in the dim light, yet her eyes, blazing with an unearthly fire, bore into Maria. Her tongue, stained with fresh blood, hung from her mouth, and her hair was wild, tangled all the way down to the floor.

By the sound of her own guttural scream, Sister Maria was jolted awake. She shot upright in her bed, skin damp with perspiration. She stumbled out of bed and toward the switch on the wall. The light revealed her familiar bedroom, but her heart continued to beat rapidly. She hesitated for a few moments, standing by the door, collecting her thoughts. *It's just a dream.*

The following morning held a series of unexpected twists for Sister Maria. Anticipating a firm reprimand when she approached Revered Mother, she was taken aback to instead receive curt directions to visit Father Patrick, accompanied by a neatly folded note detailing where to meet him. Sister Maria quickly thanked Revered Mother and arranged for a colleague to cover her upcoming class.

She headed to Father Patrick's office at nearby Saint Joseph's Academy. When she entered, she noticed the chaotic spread of papers across his desk, presumably transfers he handled for the Loreto Order. He had white hair and piercing blue eyes. He gestured for her to sit, clearing a small space amidst the paper clutter for their discussion.

"I've been in Darjeeling a long time, much like yourself," he began, his voice carrying a hint of an Irish lilt. "Few sisters request to leave their order, especially not the ones who come here." She waited, feeling the weight of his scrutiny.

"Do you have news for me, Father?" He nodded slowly, retrieving a sealed white envelope from a drawer.

"Your request is granted, Sister. This contains your ticket and the details for joining the Missionaries of Charity. The travel arrangements are all sorted."

"Thank you, Father," she responded, her relief evident as she pressed her palms together. Father Patrick raised an eyebrow at the fervency of her gratitude as she eagerly took the envelope.

"Darjeeling might feel like heaven compared to what awaits you in Kolkata," he cautioned, alluding to the stark difference between the two places, and her decision to live amongst the squalor.

"I'm ready to forgo certain luxuries," she replied confidently.

"They told me you screamed at the father of one of your students—threatened to beat him and dragged him out of the school. Is that true?"

She paused, her expression revealing a touch of remorse.

"Yes, Father."

"It seems that incident hastened your transfer. Do you believe such behavior is fitting for someone in your position?"

"No, Father."

"Good. Because Calcutta is not without its sordid people, and you won't be able to fight them all yourself. Even their goddess has a fierce side."

10.

ARYA WOKE UP feeling better than she had in weeks. She had a chai in the courtyard early in the morning and greeted Babu on her way out. This time, instead of heading to the Sister House in the morning, Arya figured out the way to the train station on foot, and then rode the handful of stops to Kalighat station. From there, she proceeded the short distance to Nirmal Hriday.

The sun streamed through the slender windows, casting patterns on the wall. Sister Maria stood in front of the door, giving a few new volunteers the briefing. Arya gave her a brief nod and got straight to work. Just like the day before, she helped prepare large batches of rice and curry with the other volunteers, and at lunchtime, hauled heavy pots downstairs, serving food to everyone in her section.

After lunch cleanup, Arya found herself idly observing Sister Maria in the office as she organized medications. The cabinets, surprisingly unlocked, sparked Arya's curiosity about the types of pills they might contain. She covertly watched Sister Maria, who was absorbed in methodically dispensing pills into paper cups and marking them with bed numbers. Arya flirted with the notion of stealing some to get high, the temptation lingering in her mind. A sudden strange noise from across the hall snapped her back to reality.

From the far end of the hall, a man abruptly began yelling. With untamed hair and a thick gray beard, he suddenly jumped onto his bed, continuing his shouts, seemingly lost in a bout of psychosis. His heightened agitation and aggressive demeanor scared the people around him.

"Sister Josephine, it's Prakash!" came a shout from the office. Almost immediately, Sister Josephine sprinted downstairs, a concerned frown etched on her face.

"What's going on with him?" Arya inquired, noting the evident distress on the nuns' faces.

"He's mentally unstable," Sister Maria explained hastily. "We need to administer a sedative, or he'll become even more agitated."

Some volunteers from Prakash's end of the hall quickly distanced themselves, while patients in adjacent beds tried to make themselves inconspicuous, avoiding any interaction with the agitated man. Unfazed by the potential for a physical confrontation, Arya calmly made her way to the other end of the hall, pausing a short distance from Prakash's bed. She then approached slowly and deliberately, aiming to avoid any sudden movements that might alarm him further.

"Watch out!" Sister Maria yelled.

Arya was too close. Prakash, provoked by her nearness, jumped off the bed and swung wildly at her. She ducked under his fist, and he lost his footing, crashing to the floor. He sprang back to his feet and charged at her again. Arya didn't hesitate, stepping forward, and punching him square on the bridge of the nose. He went down with a thud. This time, she was on him, pinning him to the ground with her knee on his back and twisting one of his arms behind him. He screamed and spat, rambling nonsense and obscenities, trying to wriggle out.

"I have him!" Arya called out to Sister Maria.

"Hold him steady!" Sister Maria ordered, racing over with a syringe at the ready. Without hesitation, she kneeled and administered the shot to Prakash's thigh. Almost immediately, his frenetic thrashing slowed. Sensing the change, Arya released her grip, and Prakash sprawled out, limp and sedated. Sister Josephine, with the aid of a volunteer, helped Sister Maria move the now subdued Prakash back to bed. He lay there, breathing evenly, one eye half-open in a drowsy gaze.

Catching her breath, Arya inquired, "What did you give him?"

"Valium," responded Sister Maria, heading back to the small office. She paused, turning to look at Arya. "You didn't flinch, even when he swung at you."

"I used to box," Arya shrugged, following her back to the office.

Arya's eyes were drawn to the fresh batch of medications on the table as she entered the office. Sister Josephine was busy sorting them. Almost without realizing it, Arya reached out and picked up a box. "Codeine," she read. She hesitated, her mind calculating how much she'd need to get really high. She took a deep breath, trying to shake off the temptation.

"Are you feeling alright?" She found herself locked in Sister Maria's perceptive gaze.

"Yes," she replied, quickly handing the box over. Sister Maria took the box from her hands and, without breaking eye contact, beamed a look of warmth and empathy at Arya.

"I noticed," she began softly, nodding toward the faint track marks on Arya's arm. Arya's reflex was to cover them up, embarrassment flooding her cheeks. Sensing the unease, Sister Maria gracefully shifted the topic. "Have you made any friends here?"

"I met the drunk boxer on the roof, but I wouldn't call him a friend."

"Ah, Philip."

"You're familiar with him?"

"He's crossed our path a few times."

"And he doesn't volunteer here?"

"He's never shown interest."

"Why does he hang around, then?"

"You'd have to ask him," Sister Maria responded thoughtfully. "Perhaps you'll be the one he finally opens up to. Faith hasn't been his guiding light."

After finishing her second shift duties, Arya headed out. She walked through Kolkata's busy streets, passing by vendors and rickshaws. Catching the train from Kalighat to Chowringhee, she took the familiar route back to Sudder Street.

She returned to the hostel around seven and went up to her room to change before coming back down for some food. As she walked past the top of the stairs, she heard Philip's shadowboxing sounds, echoing, "esh… esh… esh…," from the rooftop. Despite being tempted to go up and watch, she proceeded downwards and found a place to sit in the courtyard where Chaiwallah could bring her something to eat.

Arya took a moment to survey the courtyard, picking out some familiar faces from Nirmal Hriday. They were deep in an animated Spanish conversation, laughing and sharing stories. Close by, two Asian men she hadn't met before were intently playing cards. They smiled in her direction when their eyes met hers.

"What are you playing?" she asked.

"Five card poker," the one with a messy bun shouted back. "Wanna join?"

"Sure," she said, sliding into the vacant chair beside them.

"My name is Jun. This is Hiro," he said, introducing his friend. "We're from Japan."

"I'm Arya."

Arya handed Jun 500 rupees, in return for which he slid her a handful of worn-out bottle caps—their makeshift poker chips for the night. The cards were old, the edges frayed and darkened from use. As the game progressed, the air filled with light banter, interspersed with street noises, and the distant hum of Kolkata's night. For the next two hours, they enjoyed each other's company. Though she lost every round, Arya was glad for the company—she even had a smile on her face.

Over the course of the following week, Arya became increasingly immersed in her volunteer work at Nirmal Hriday. She kept a respectful distance from Philip and continued to find new ways to help Sister Maria and the patients. She also picked up on nuances she'd missed early on. Some volunteers only visited once; others had been there for months. The patients spoke multiple languages, not just English and Bengali. More experienced volunteers were better at connecting without language, using gestures and eye contact to communicate and be understood.

Away from her volunteer work, Arya found herself getting used to Kolkata's relentless pulse, the constant hum of the city, the daily encounters with beggars— children smeared with grime, elderly men in tattered clothes, mothers cradling babies and pleading for enough money to afford powdered milk. These scenes etched themselves into her daily life, becoming as much a part of her routine as the work she did at Nirmal Hriday.

The hostel, too, began to feel more comfortable, particularly after a few more laid-back poker nights with Jun and Hiro. Wanting to make her space more personal, she picked up a colorful painting at one of the markets, where she was improving at bargaining. It was a small, vibrant painting of Kali, portrayed with dark skin, four arms, fiery red eyes, and a tongue that curled with ferocity. Compelled by its boldness and nostalgia for her father, she made a spot for it on her wall.

"Look at Little Kali now," she whispered to herself as she hammered the nail with a stone from outside.

But amidst her gradual adjustment to the city's rhythm, what struck Arya the most was the unwavering dedication of the nuns. Day after day, they were the first to arrive and the last to leave; their commitment extending well beyond simply managing the volunteers. They were hands-on in every facet of service, from seeking out those in need to providing meals, hygiene, medical care, and above all, ensuring each individual was treated with profound dignity.

One evening, during the second shift, as Arya was gathering used plates from beside the cots of recuperating patients to take upstairs for washing, she witnessed an unexpected arrival…a young priest. In his arms, he carefully cradled a frail elderly woman, her body limp, seemingly lifeless. He looked around, his eyes searching for assistance.

"Please. Help. Please. I found her outside the hospital. Rats were feeding on her feet," he announced. His voice was tinged with a Polish accent.

"Bring her in!" Sister Maria cried out, leading the priest to one of the few empty beds near the entrance. "I will look after her."

After ensuring the elderly woman was as comfortable as possible, Sister Maria escorted the priest to the door. She then hurried to get a refreshing glass of water, and even though the woman seemed too frail to eat, Sister Maria still asked Sister Josephine to prepare a light, nourishing meal.

Sisters Maria and Josephine worked in tandem, gently tending to the old woman. They carefully disinfected her injuries, meticulously cleansing her skin with a damp cloth, showing a combination of expertise and compassion. Observing their efforts, Arya felt compelled to stay and assist, given the sudden and unexpected turn of events.

But Sister Maria, sensing Arya's intention, gave her a reassuring smile.

"Thank you, Arya, but you've done plenty today. Get some rest, and we'll see you tomorrow," she said, subtly conveying her gratitude.

On her way to the train station, Arya was in awe of the nuns even more. They dedicated themselves to helping the poor, approaching every act of service, no matter how large or small, with unwavering commitment. On the train, her thoughts wandered to the documentary at Terrance's place. It seemed like it had been an omen.

Stepping off the train and making her way back to the hostel, the streets were empty and quiet, except for the countless homeless sleeping on the streets. A sudden, sharp scream from across the street jolted Arya from her thoughts.

A young woman, no more than twenty years old, wearing a bright yellow and gold sari, burst out of the entrance to an apartment building and started sprinting down the street with two men trailing her closely. They quickly caught up to her, cornering her against a building's wall. A few pedestrians further down the street quickened their steps, opting to avoid getting involved.

"Leave her alone!" Arya yelled, racing across the street. The men turned and stared angrily. One of them shouted something in Bengali, clearly cursing at her, and she could see the fear in the young woman's eyes.

"Leave now!" the other man barked at her, speaking English. He advanced, and Arya stood her ground. He was taller and looked menacing, dressed in all black. The young woman pinned to the wall squirmed in his friend's grasp, pleading to be set free, and she caught a swift, harsh slap across her face.

"Stop!" Arya shouted, shoving the man in front of her. He swung violently towards her, but Arya dodged, countering with a brutal punch straight to his nose. He hit the pavement with a thud.

"Crazy bitch!" the other shouted, releasing the woman and charging at Arya. He was stocky and moved with a raw aggression. She capitalized on her height advantage, landing two swift jabs that split the skin above his eye. A solid right hook followed, sending him down next to his friend.

"Run!" Arya commanded. The woman grabbed her sari and took off running down the street. Arya watched as she vanished out of sight and then ran in the opposite direction, making her way back to the hostel.

11.

WHEN ARYA GOT out of bed in the morning, her knuckles were bruised and sore. She grinned in satisfaction, recalling the altercation and her good deed. After taking a shower, she went downstairs for some chai in the courtyard, threw away the last of her cigarettes, and then went off to volunteer. At Nirmal Hriday, Sisters Maria and Josephine were already hard at work getting the hall ready. Arya scanned the room for the elderly woman who had been admitted just hours ago, but she was no longer in her bed.

"Where is she?" Arya asked Sister Maria, as she passed by the small office.

"She died last night." Arya paused for a moment, trying to find the right words to say. "It's alright, dear. She was not alone, and this is the work we do."

"Did you get any rest last night?" Arya asked.

"A little bit..." Sister Maria said, brushing it off. "Now hurry up and start your duties because I have something else in store for you later on."

Jumping into her shift, Arya went up to the kitchen and received instructions from Sister Josephine on how to prepare a new green curry for lunch. She dove straight into the kitchen's organized chaos, using a worn-out knife to chop vegetables and direct other volunteers through their respective duties.

After the last plate from lunch was cleaned and stored, Sister Maria called Arya to a specific patient's bed. It was Bishal. He lay there, cradling his swollen belly, letting out low moans of agony. Sister Maria handed Arya a jar of therapeutic ointment and demonstrated the gentle method of applying it to Bishal's distended abdomen, aiming to alleviate some of his pain. She stayed with him that afternoon, skipping her dinnertime chores to tend to him.

By the end of the night, his breathing had slowed down considerably. Arya gently persisted with the ointment, her hands moving in rhythmic circles, even as the pauses between his breaths lengthened. And then, in a moment that seemed suspended in time, his once desperate gasps ceased altogether. The last time she had been this close to death, it had been her father.

"He's at peace now," Sister Maria said, breaking the silence. Arya looked up to find Sister Maria's warm eyes fixed on Bishal. "You gave him a comfort many can't find in their last moments."

"Did it make a difference?" Arya asked, seeking affirmation.

"You showed him compassion. You gave him dignity in death." Arya sealed the jar of ointment and rose to her feet. Sister Maria held out her hand, and Arya took it hesitantly. The nun recited a brief prayer, but it was the closing line that resonated differently.

"A beautiful death is for people who lived like animals to die like angels—loved and wanted."

"I like that," Arya said, turning to look at her.

"It was Mother Teresa who said that."

They stood in silence for a few moments, and the atmosphere in the room shifted. The sounds of shuffling feet and whispered conversations dwindled, replaced by a weighty silence. The men in the adjacent beds lowered their heads to show respect. In the background, the faint murmur of Sister Josephine's voice could be heard as she spoke from the small office. Shortly thereafter, funerary workers came to take the body away.

"Where will he be buried?" Arya asked.

"It will be a cremation, since he was Hindu," Sister Maria said as she lightly patted Arya's shoulder. "We honor their burial traditions and use our own when the deceased are Christian. But most of those we receive here are Hindus and Buddhists."

At the end of another long day, Arya left the hospice with an understanding that the nuns cared more about treating people with dignity than forcing ideology. Arriving back at the hostel, Arya felt the urge to relax and enjoy another game of poker with Jun and Hiro. She went to her room to freshen up and change her clothes, planning to wait for them afterward in the courtyard.

On her way down, Arya paused for a moment to listen for the sound of Philip shadowboxing. She was met with silence. Curiosity getting the better of her, she went up to see if he was there and found him sitting at the corner of the rooftop, smoking a cigarette, a half-full bottle of whiskey on the table.

"Fuck off!" he grunted when he saw her head pop over the top of the stairs. She ignored the comment and walked right up to his table.

"I'm a recovering drug addict." Philip just stared at her expressionless until Arya broke the silence.

"Why are you here?" That was the question everyone seemed to wonder but that Philip couldn't bring himself to answer.

"Why not here? It's cheap, and if I drink enough, I don't notice how bloody nasty the place is—it's just like Paris. But why are you here?" With nowhere to sit, Arya rested against the railing, her back to the bustling street below. "You don't seem like the kind of person who comes to Kolkata," he pressed, glancing at the bruising on her knuckles.

"My father was from here, but I came to get away from the mess I made of my life in NY."

"Why do you care about boxing so much?" he asked, slightly intrigued by this edgy young woman, unlike any of the other volunteers at the hostel.

"I used to compete, but right now I just want to be active—you know?"

"Well, I ain't about to fight any women, so you can fuck off."

"How about you train me?"

"No. I'm no trainer."

"I'll buy your drinks," she pushed back. "Train me and you can drink for free. What else do you have to do?" Philip sipped his whiskey, looking over the railing to the street below. A choir of car horns and distant shouting echoed over the city.

Arya's presence was an anomaly in his carefully guarded solitude. He watched her for a moment, her gaze fixed on him, her hands fidgeting as she waited for his verdict. She held her breath for a stranger's judgment. He didn't know the full weight of her request—that boxing wasn't just a sport, but a lifeline pulling her from the depths of hell.

"Show me your boxing stance."

Arya pushed away from the railing, positioned her feet sideways, and raised her fists.

"Stand at an angle, don't square up like that." Philip stood up and grabbed Arya's shoulders, rotating her sideways. "Good," he said, stepping away. "Give me some ones and twos."

She showed her technique, throwing jabs and crosses, alternating her hips.

"Great," he said, putting the cap on his bottle of whiskey. "I could go for a beer." He sat back down and looked at her. Arya chuckled and headed downstairs to tell Chaiwallah the next one was on her. Once back, Philip guided her through shadowboxing drills, enough for Arya to work up a sweat.

The next day, Arya arrived at Nirmal Hriday in a good mood and navigated her way through the morning shift. With Sister Josephine preoccupied with the new admissions brought in by the priests, she sought to help, jumping in to direct volunteers to their duties, oversee the kitchen, and assist newcomers that appeared worried or confused. It was a whirlwind, and it wasn't until after lunch that she had a moment to catch up with Sister Maria in the small office. During their conversation, Sister Maria shared a piece of news that took Arya by surprise.

"Starting next week, I'm going to be rotating to our school for orphans—Karuna Dan."

"I thought you managed things here—"

"I've been a teacher in the past, so my roles within the mission are varied," Sister Maria said, while sorting out the day's medications. Arya's gaze briefly lingered on the box of codeine.

"Do I just keep coming when you're not here?"

"You are welcome to continue volunteering here. Sister Josephine appreciates your hard work. But I'd like you to come with me," Sister Maria said. "I think it would be good for you to be around the children. I miss them myself."

"How old are they?"

"I teach an older class, but Sister Catherine could use a hand with the first grade. There are things I need to address before I transfer. Give me a few days, and I'll send word to Babu for you to come."

Throughout the second half of the day, Arya felt a growing sense of dread, recalling how easily her mind had spiraled with too much free time.

That evening, Arya found Philip on the roof again as she carried two cold beers from Chaiwallah and placed them on his table. He cracked the first one open, and they resumed training. As she warmed up, Arya felt old reflexes kicking into gear. Philip, picking up on this change, intensified her session, adding new combinations and drills for her to execute. By the end of their 40-minute session, she was out of breath and drenched in sweat.

"I'm not going to see the nuns for a couple of days. I'm waiting to hear where they want me to volunteer next, and I'm worried about too much free time. Any chance we could do another session during the day?" Arya was certain Philip would shoot her down.

"Come up tomorrow around noon. We'll see," Philip said aloofly.

When she climbed to the roof the next day at noon, she found Philip already there, a collection of boxing gear spread out, catching the midday heat—training gloves, wraps, pads, a jump rope, and a mat for ab work.

Philip delved deep into the techniques, starting off with foundational combinations before progressing to trickier ones. After making Arya shadowbox for a good fifteen minutes, he tossed her the gloves and pulled out the pads. They danced across the rooftop for twenty minutes—Arya snapping punches on target, while

Philip maneuvered the pads, making her duck and weave.

"Get your hands up and stop leaning forward," he coached, in-between punches. Philip led Arya around the roof, moving with ease until suddenly his right leg buckled underneath him. He got up quickly and resumed his position, limping slightly.

"Are you okay?"

"It's fine."

"But you're—"

"I'm good. Fetch me a cold beer, will you?"

Arya rolled her eyes and went downstairs to get it.

12.

AS THE SUN began its descent over Kolkata, two police constables, dressed in crisp white uniforms, stepped into a nondescript jewelry store in the heart of the city. Dim lighting obscured the window displays, and a security grill was drawn halfway down, adding to the store's discreet appearance. Only the sign hanging above the entrance, "G.K. Jewelers," gave any hint of what was inside, hidden from prying eyes.

The room was heavy with the smell of cigarettes and hashish. A display table, with jewelry haphazardly arranged under a glass cover, sat in the center of the room. The constables' eyes briefly darted to a few standout pieces as they moved deeper into the store.

"Sit," Garu grunted from his desk.

They seated themselves across from him, watching as he slid a substantial gold necklace, set with red and white stones, to the side. In the corner, near the door leading to the back stairwell, his right-hand man stood silently, casting an ominous shadow over the room.

Garu sized up the constables with a hardened glare, his fat neck turning slightly as he assessed each man. They'd lurked outside his store multiple times that week, feigning courtesy, posing as guardians of business safety. But their intention was to manipulate or shake down prosperous businesses for a payoff, a well-known practice among Kolkata's shadier law enforcers.

Yet, Garu knew their game. Holding the cards in his favor, their obvious greed only made him smirk. To him, control was everything, and money was just another way to keep them in line. It all came down to what they'd agree to do for him.

"This is one of my three businesses. My father was not a rich man, and neither are you. But I am." Garu laughed.

The constables exchanged a fleeting, uneasy look. Though the two looked somewhat alike, with matching thick mustaches shadowing their lips, their statures differed—one lean and wiry, the other more compact and thicker around the waist.

"Yessir. We have heard about you," the tall one muttered nervously.

"If we are to come to an arrangement, it is for my other businesses. You understand? I don't need you here." He gestured at the empty store.

"Other businesses?" the constable ventured, his voice edged with caution.

His partner shifted uneasily. They already knew that Garu trafficked women among other shady ventures.

"Sandeep, get the packages," Garu said.

Without a word, Sandeep moved from his spot, disappearing through the back door to the apartment above. Moments later, he returned, setting a brown envelope before each man. They cracked open the seals to look at the money inside, sharing a look of astonishment, then turned their attention back to Garu, nodding in agreement.

"Women sell better than jewelry. And you can sell them many times," Garu said. "I have two places. One in Sonagachi, but you'll be watching the one in Bhowanipore. Sometimes, the women act up, my customers get rough, and the neighbors call the police. I don't want to deal with these headaches when they happen."

"Who are the customers?" the stockier constable asked.

"College boys, lawyers, married men, taxi drivers, poor police constables… Does it matter?" Garu snapped.

"No sir," the taller one interjected, ignoring the thinly veiled insult and trying to prevent another stupid question.

"My other business…" Garu continued. "Have you ever been to a boxing match?"

"No," they answered in unison.

"You will see one soon. Kolkata has a rich boxing tradition, and Sandeep is one of my champions. Men with money buy whores and they gamble. My fight club pulls in a lot of money, and it is all in cash. I need better security and police presence."

"It is a lot of work for us to protect two businesses," one of the constables said, trying to sound confident, fishing for what else may be offered. Sandeep, who had been watching from the corner, stepped forward again and loomed over the constables. Garu smiled because negotiation was a good sign. It meant he'd already bought them. He had already handed them the envelopes with a third of their yearly salaries inside. He trusted that greed would prevail.

"I have given you a large amount of money in good faith," Garu replied, picking up the necklace on his desk to feel the weight in his hands. The diamonds and gold sparkled in the dim light. "This piece is worth more than both of you combined. Don't be stupid." With Sandeep glaring down, neither constable felt comfortable enough to ask for more money. Ever since Garu had hired him at age twenty, he'd come to rely on Sandeep to get the results he wanted in negotiations.

"No one will interfere with your business," the constable declared at last, relinquishing his authority in the discussion. The smaller partner, who had been attempting to appear intelligent, nodded in agreement to indicate he was pleased with the arrangement as it stood.

"Good news," Garu declared, just as another one of his men came through the door with a young girl. Nurul was young, in his mid-twenties, a few years younger than Sandeep, with a greasy mop on his head. Walking ahead of him was the girl, no older than twelve. She had dark skin and long black hair, tangled down to her waist. Too young for a sari, she wore boys' clothes, and tears streamed down her face.

"She wants to go back to Bangladesh," Nurul scoffed, showing no sympathy for the frightened girl. The constables were taken aback but kept their silence.

"You may go now," Garu said in a stern voice, motioning for them to stand up. "I will contact you later." They left quickly, fumbling to tuck the envelopes discreetly into their pockets.

"Come, come, Yunni," Garu said, waving the young girl over. Nurul pushed her toward Garu, who grasped Yunni's little face, studying her features intently.

"Should we take her to Songachi?" Nurul inquired. Sonagachi was the easiest place, in the middle of the red-light district, where Sandeep and Nurul would have expected Garu to hide her, though he had the other place in the residential and subdued neighborhood of Bhowanipore.

"No, Bhowanipore," Garu snapped, his newfound alliance with the police boosting his confidence. "She will be my top earner, and she will not stand out in a place already full of whores."

"But she will be noticed—"

"She will be noticed, and she will be eaten," Garu said. "I will take her myself."

Garu called the driver. When his car arrived, they quickly ushered Yunni into the back of the sedan between Nurul and Sandeep. They arrived twenty minutes later. The Bhowanipore brothel was on a quiet street, situated between other small two-story dwellings.

Once Yunni was through the door, all eyes were on her. The dimly lit hallway stretched out, doors leading off to who knows where. Faces peeked out, women with tired eyes sizing her up. Garu grabbed her arm, pulled her upstairs, and shoved her into a room.

The room had three walls lined with beds, a dresser standing in the corner, and a closet. On the bed sat a woman in a yellow sari, a long braid running down her back. She was casually watching a video on her phone, caught off guard by the unexpected entrance.

"Bimala, this is Yunni. You will prepare her," Garu ordered, pushing the girl forward. The young woman shot up, startled but now sharply aware of who was speaking to her. Yunni stepped forward eagerly, happy to get away from Garu. She came forward and clasped on to Bimala's waist, burying her face in the fabric of the sari.

"She's very young," Bimala said, looking down at the girl. "I think she—"

"Shut up!" Garu shouted, slapping Bimala across the cheek. "Do not question me." Too intimidated to speak up once more, she embraced the child and averted her gaze.

"The man who found her told her family she would marry a prince. There is no prince—you know that. She will work for me, and you will teach her what she needs to know."

"Yes, sir," Bimala murmured.

"Tell her we will buy her new clothes to celebrate Durga Puja," Garu said mockingly, walking out of the room.

Two of the women from down the hallway came to the door, peering in to get a better look at the new girl. Bimala ran a wet cloth over Yunni's face and body, wiping the dirt and tears away. She spent a few hours combing her hair, working out all the knots.

"We take care of each other," she said, trying to comfort the girl.

"I want to see my family."

"This is your family."

"I don't want this—"

"Shhh. You'll get used to it."

13.

AFTER FIVE HARD days of serious boxing, Arya felt her relationship with Philip evolving, inching closer to genuine friendship. One evening, following an especially tough workout, Arya paused to collect herself. Drawing a deep breath, she shared with Philip the incident from a few weeks ago, detailing her encounter with two men who were harassing a young woman on the street, and then mentioned how she'd taken each one down with one punch each.

"You knocked them both down?" Philip asked, eager for the story.

"Yeah."

"Do you know who they were?"

"Just two losers from the street, who cares—"

Philip grinned. "Must've felt pretty great."

"It did."

"You see them again?"

"Nope."

That night, after a refreshing shower, Arya pulled out her stash of money from its secret spot in her luggage and recounted it, not once, but multiple times. She mentally calculated how long she could afford to stay in Kolkata based on her current budget. The withdrawal was behind her, and as the cravings continued to subside, she considered the idea of staying long term. By her estimation, if she was frugal, she had enough for six months. And that budget had no room for relapses.

After her late sessions, Arya would retreat to her room for the night. But after morning workouts, she felt a restless drive to occupy the time she had spent volunteering. She roamed the neighborhood around the hostel and delved into tattered books left by previous volunteers in the courtyard. Days had blurred since her last cigarette, and she was resolute about giving up smoking, though the urge remained.

On day six, Philip put Arya through a grueling morning conditioning session—a mix of interval footwork drills, jump rope, and calisthenics. Exhausted, she headed back to her room and found a note tacked to her door. It was from Babu, detailing the time and place where she was to meet Sister Maria the next day, at one of the Missionaries of Charity's orphanage schools.

That evening, Philip focused on pad work, honing Arya's punching and defensive skills. As she moved, Arya talked a little of her past as a fighter—competing in regional tournaments under Coach Greg, and brawling for cash at underground fight clubs.

"I knew you weren't the volunteer type," Philip said, moving the pads, making them harder to hit. "Bet you weren't too bad neither."

She landed a solid punch, her eyes never leaving the target. "Know any places around here I can fight?"

"Why would you want to do that?"

She dodged a swing of the pad and counterpunched. "Eventually, I'll be out of cash, and I'll need a way to earn."

"I don't think they let women fight here," Philip said, unaware of Kolkata's long-standing boxing history.

"You ever worry about money?" she asked, throwing a couple of quick jabs.

"I stay in this shit hole, so I don't have to."

She paused, lowering her gloves. "And when the money does run out?"

"I figured I'd be gone too."

After wrapping up, Arya headed downstairs and bought a cold beer from Chaiwallah. Not as payment for the training, but as a gesture. Handing it to Philip, she realized it was the first time she truly glimpsed the depth of his brokenness.

In the morning, Arya discovered that reaching the Karuna Dan school was considerably simpler than navigating her way to Nirmal Hriday. Located in the neighboring area of Bhowanipore, it was just a short autorickshaw ride away. Handing over forty rupees, she was whisked through bustling main streets before tapering off into the more serene residential lanes. The school was set back behind a tall cement barrier, anchored by a set of twin wooden gates. The horizontal planks of each gate were painted green, with just enough space between them to see who was on the other side.

Drawing closer, Arya spotted Sister Maria poised on the opposite side of the gate, ready to greet her. With a welcoming gesture, Sister Maria unlatched the gate, letting her in.

"Welcome," Sister Maria greeted, motioning Arya inside. "I apologize for the wait. I had matters to attend to at another school before coming here. Did you end up getting to know Philip any better?"

"He's hard to get to know…but he agreed to do some boxing training with me."

Sister Maria's face went blank. "He's been through a lot… but I've always believed he has a good heart. Perhaps this act of service to you will open up his heart in the way that he needs."

"Or the whiskey and beer will," Arya joked.

Sister Maria gestured for her to come forward. Once inside, Arya's eyes were drawn to a playground area. Swings, slides, and monkey bars sat atop a patch of bare ground, and beyond, a paved courtyard with benches stretched out in front of the single-story school building.

A cheerful nun in a white sari with blue stripes hurried over, holding a young girl with pigtails, who looked about five or six years old.

"Here's someone who couldn't wait for your return," Sister Catherine said with a smile, nudging the girl gently towards Sister Maria, who kneeled down.

"Did you miss me, Gita?" The girl nodded, her eyes bright.

"Are you back?"

"Yes," Sister Maria replied. "And there's someone I want to introduce you to. Gita, this is my friend, Arya," she said, turning to her.

"Hi, Gita!" Arya said, her voice friendly and inviting.

"Hello, Arya," Gita replied in a shy whisper.

"How old are you?"

"Six."

"Wow. Six years old."

"She's one of our little angels," Sister Maria said, carrying her over toward the playground. "You'll be working with her class, the first grade. Go on, go play for a few minutes before class," she told Gita.

The playground was alive with the energy of dozens of children, taking full advantage of the fleeting moments of freedom before the morning bell. From atop the jungle gym, a boy about Gita's age clambered down and rushed to greet her. Without a word, he took her hand, leading her to one of the platforms. Side by side, they climbed and settled at the top, their tiny feet swinging in the air.

"That's very sweet," Arya said.

"That's Podip. He and Gita share a unique bond."

Arya gave her a puzzled look.

Sister Maria took a few steps back and lowered her voice. "Same with any of our homes. The sisters and priests find abandoned children on the streets, and we bring them here. I brought Gita and Podip myself."

"Really? From where?"

Sister Maria hesitated momentarily, then motioned for Arya to follow her. She walked back to the green gate, opened it, and took a few steps outside into the street.

"I rescued them from there," she said, pointing down the street at a building in the distance.

"What's that?"

"It's a brothel," Sister Maria said, her eyes clouded with a twinge of anger. "At Karuna Dan, we currently have over thirty children. Many, like Gita and Podip, were born to those women. The mothers agree to have their children educated here, visiting when they can. They are poor women and have no other means for money other than to be prostitutes."

"You don't work directly with them?"

"The women don't want us interfering in their lives."

"Gita and Podip's mothers are there now?"

"Gita's mother is no longer there, but Podip's mother still is. We're just glad we got to the children before they got pulled into that world."

"They sell children here?" Arya whispered, eyes wide with disbelief.

"Child prostitution is common in Kolkata."

Arya looked over at Gita and Podip sitting on the bench, holding hands, inculpable in the tragedies that made them. She wished to believe life wasn't capable of such cruelty.

"What happened to Gita's mom?"

"It's been a year since she disappeared," Sister Maria replied, her voice marred by sadness. "For a time, Gita would wander outside, trying to find her. But she's stopped doing that. Our hope is someday a good family, maybe from Europe or the US, will bring both Gita and Podip together into their home."

"No one adopts them here in India?"

"Most who consider it here do not want the children of prostitutes."

When the morning bell rang, signaling the start of classes, Arya followed everyone into the school building.

"Sister Catherine will tell you what to do," Sister Maria said before she went down the hall to the fourth grade.

Arya trailed behind Gita and Podip into a sunlit classroom with windows overlooking the courtyard. She was pleasantly surprised to find Jun and Hiro there, preparing to assist Sister Catherine with first-grade math.

Arya quickly scanned the room. Kids' drawings added color to the walls, and a board showcased photos of students with their names underneath. The desks, organized in tidy rows, led her eyes to Gita and Podip sitting together at the back. She slid into the vacant seat beside them. Sister Catherine wrote a basic math equation on the chalkboard to start the class, prompting the students to jot down their solutions. Jun and Hiro moved about, peeking into notebooks and guiding where necessary.

"You are both really smart," Arya said, noticing their accurate solutions and neat handwriting.

Gita looked up, her eyes shining with interest. "Are you from America?"

"Yes, I am. What do you know about it?"

"It gets cold," Gita replied simply.

"That's right." Arya smiled. "Especially in the winter."

"I want to go there," Gita said thoughtfully. "But Podip wants to stay here."

Arya leaned in slightly, making sure not to disrupt the ongoing lesson, and whispered to Podip, "It's nice to meet you."

He offered a shy smile in return. Sister Catherine then presented another math problem, and once again, both Gita and Podip got it right.

Throughout the day, Arya stuck with Gita and Podip for three more classes. She quickly realized that working at the school felt less intense than her time at Nirmal Hriday, and the children's proficiency in English made her interactions enjoyable.

Arya headed back to the hostel with a couple of hours left before her scheduled session with Philip. As she waited in her room, her thoughts kept returning to the stories Sister Maria shared about Gita and Podip. Their close proximity to the grim reality of prostitution, especially after her own experiences in New York, bothered Arya. At least she was capable of defending herself. She tried to suppress these feelings, but they gnawed at her from within.

Arya stepped onto the rooftop to find Philip ready and waiting. They started with basic warm-ups and moved to shadowboxing. When they shifted to pad work, Philip noticed Arya's hits were harder, fueled by anger.

"One of the sisters piss you off?" Philip teased. He slipped off the pads for a moment and went over to his table for a few chugs of his beer.

"Just drink your bottle," Arya snapped back, staring at him with sudden contempt.

"You got something to say to me?"

"Doesn't it bother you being around so much suffering? Why don't you care that people are hurting around you?"

"What the fuck do you know about hurt?" He raised his voice, shattering his bottle on the ground.

"Hey, relax—"

"Get the fuck off my roof!" Realizing her words had cut much deeper than intended, Arya left the roof immediately and spent the remainder of the evening in her room.

14.

*News item from Birmingham (UK.) Weekly Gazette,
September 4, 2016:*

**MOTHER TERESA declared saint before
audience at the Vatican.**

*Mother Teresa, a Catholic nun who devoted her life
to helping India's poor, has been declared a saint in a
canonization Mass held by Pope Francis at the Vatican.*

*The Pope delivered the ceremony for the Albanian-
born nun before huge crowds gathered in Vatican City
on Sunday morning.*

PHILIP READ THE front-page story, and it brought a
bit of cheer to an otherwise cold and gloomy day. He
drove to the pub at noon to find Paulie already waiting
for him at the bar with two of his men. He joined them
on the next stool closest to the door. No other patrons
were inside. The bartender, a timid man with red hair,
brought over three pints of ale and a diet soda for Philip,
then briskly returned to the far side of the bar, out of
earshot.

Everyone in Birmingham had heard of Paulie,
including Philip, though he didn't fully understand the
implication of being invited at first. It was only after
telling a fellow fighter at the gym about the request that
he learned the true meaning of the summons—not

showing up would be taken as an insult. Reluctantly, in jeans and a sweatshirt, Philip went to the pub instead of the gym and sat next to three gangsters in tailored suits. With the way he felt going into his upcoming fight, it would've been a day best spent hibernating at home.

Paulie began speaking of his favorite matches, classic bouts that all boxing fanatics liked to reference, and Philip tuned out this quintessential dribble about "Tyson… Ali… Foreman… Lewis…" When he tuned back in, the tone and conversation had changed abruptly and were quite different.

"I need ya to go down in the fourth tomorrow, ya hear what I'm sayin?" Paulie said, lightly slapping Philip's chin.

What the fuck did he just ask me to do? Throw a fight? Like his friends had told him, Philip understood refusing would be taken as an insult. His mind raced, considering his family, his integrity, his boxing record, all in a fraction of a second. Paulie's men leaned in to stare at Philip, making his moment of deliberation as uncomfortable as possible.

This mobster is telling me what to do.

"Did you hear what I said?" Paulie emphasized.

"Go down in the fourth," Philip murmured, desperate yet unable to think of something else to say.

"It's done," Paulie said. He drank the last bit of ale in his glass, slammed it on the bar.

"Your career's done anyway, kid," Paulie said, standing up to leave. "You gotta focus on survival now."

In a moment of doubt, Paulie's words carried weight. Nearing his forties, Philip's boxing career was indeed coming to an end. He stayed for a few minutes, considering the fight ahead, thinking he'd be lucky to get knocked out in the fourth and lose the honest way. His opponent was a younger fighter from Aston Villa named Bowen with an impressive knockout ratio. It wasn't out of the question. Conflicted, Philip said nothing to his wife, Anna, that evening, or to his ten-year-old son, Dorian. After many years of living with a boxer, they'd seen his moodiness ahead of a fight enough times to know he needed space, and at Philip's suggestion, Anna wasn't planning to go to the match.

"You feel alright about this one?" she asked, sensing trepidation in Philip's voice that night.

"He's a strong lad, but he's green in the ring," he said about his opponent, deflecting.

Using the fight as a reason to spend some time alone, Philip excused himself and went to hide in the bedroom. He stood in front of the mirror, struggling to visualize the fight as he often did, allowing worry to distract his focus.

The following night, fresh and clean shaven, Philip went under the bright lights for his 40th professional bout. He knew his corner man from prior fights, but he'd even fought at this venue before. The walkout went by in a flash, and when the pomp and music ended, Philip prepared for battle, though he had surrender on his mind.

In the first round, Bowen came out swinging, fighting his age and expending energy too soon. Going against instinct, to let the kid punch himself out, Philip engaged, and they clashed toe-to-toe in the first round. With neither fighter landing solidly, Bowen adjusted his pace and slowed down in rounds two and three. But it didn't prevent him from landing a few hard shots on Philip—wild gambles that paid off.

By the fourth round, Philip was tired of carrying Bowen, holding back the impulse to hurt him. He saw a punch coming and let it be the one. It smashed into the side of his face, and Philip dropped to the canvas.

The referee started his count as Bowen triumphantly danced away.

"One… two… three… four… five…"

"Atta-boy," Paulie laughed with his men, several rows back from ringside.

"Six… seven…"

Philip crawled to his knees and stood up before the referee counted to nine.

"Do you want to continue?" the referee asked, holding his gloves, and looking into his eyes.

"Yes," he said, breathing heavily through a bloody mouthguard.

When the referee let go, Philip banged his gloves together, signaling to the crowd and to himself that he was not finished.

"Fight!" The referee declared, releasing him to Bowen.

"What the fuck is this chump doing?" Paulie cursed, shifting in his seat.

Bowen came forward swinging like he did in the first round, looking for an easy win. Philip evaded and blocked all the advances, then dug his heels into the canvas and started moving him back with double jabs with hard rights down the middle, stunning the young man. Toe-to-toe, Philip leaned on his skills to dominate Bowen, and with half a minute left in the round, fired a left hook that put him down.

Philip gazed into the crowd through blinding lights, fearful to see Paulie's face. He expected to meet them lurking in the locker room to stab him in the gut, but no one came. He entertained worse thoughts outside the venue, expecting Paulie's men to shoot him from a passing car. Fans and spectators filed out onto the sidewalk, but Paulie and his men weren't there either.

Philip returned home to Birmingham in the back of a town car, holding an ice pack over his black eye. He checked his cellphone with the other eye to see if he had missed any calls. Seeing none, he sent a message to Anna.

I won.

No response.

By the time he made it home, Anna's and Dorian's bodies were already laying on the kitchen floor in a puddle of blood. Paulie stood beside his man from the pub, who held the silencer pistol in his hand.

Out of sheer impulse and horror, Philip charged. He managed to wrestle the gun away from him and fire two rounds into his stomach at close range, killing him instantly. A few feet away, Paulie fumbled for the weapon under his jacket and managed to fire one shot from his 9mm into Philip's leg. In retaliation, Philip emptied the rest of the clip at his chest, catapulting him into the china cabinet. Paulie's lifeless body crashed to the floor in a pile of broken porcelain and glass.

With blood gushing from his leg, Philip slowly lowered himself onto his knees, in between the bodies of his wife and son. He cradled his wife and son's faces in his hands. The sorrow was too enormous to cry. He pushed it all down and called the police. The paramedics came too, but it was too late.

Philip was loosely cuffed, hands in front, and placed into the back of the police car headed for the West Midlands Police station for questioning. Sounds were muted the way they were after fights, and he could barely hear the officer's questions coming across the metal desk.

"Why were they at your home?"

"Paulie wanted me to throw the fight. I didn't."

"Did you shoot him and his associate?"

"Yes."

"What were they doing in your home?"

"They killed my wife and son," Philip answered through tight-pressed lips, begging the detective would say something stupid.

Several hours of questions and paperwork led to the determination that Philip's actions were a clear case of self-defense, following the tragic murder of his wife and son.

Exoneration was hardly a cause for celebration. Over the next several months, aided by whiskey and self-disgust, Philip sold the furniture, the car, the house, and placed everything else into storage. Triggers and mechanisms kicked into gear, depositing life insurance money into his bank account he'd never hoped to receive. Shortly thereafter, he made plans to leave.

He boarded the plane with nothing more than a passport, a backpack, and one medium-sized suitcase half-filled with clothes. He wished to leave behind everything familiar, everything comfortable, and everything that reminded him of them. As a man who once had faith, Philip could not choose suicide, so he resigned to live out the rest of his life in self-imposed exile.

The ritual stayed the same, no matter where he was. He wandered, stumbled upon cheap places to stay, and kept drinking until nothing mattered anymore. Ignoring the occasional invitations to connect, Philip made no friends, and avoided any semblance of life or community. Seeking to match the loneliness in his heart with his surroundings, Philip turned his attention to the more foreign destinations of Southeast Asia, where he could rent a room for about the same as two pints of ale at a Birmingham pub. Unlike most of the travelers he brushed up against, attracted by exotic destinations and white sand beaches, Philip found that his guilt would not allow him to enjoy the splendors of Thailand, Cambodia, and Vietnam.

As soon as he arrived in India, Philip thought about leaving, but the squalor, poverty, and pollution of the urban centers felt like the beating he deserved. He started his journey through the subcontinent traveling south from Mumbai to Goa, where he discovered Fenny, a moonshine-type liquor made from cashews that kept him drunk while traveling up the coasts of Tamil Nadu, Andhra Pradesh, and Orissa, finally stopping in West Bengal. It was monsoon season in Kolkata when he got there. Travel had done little to heal his heart, and the rains did little to wash away the pain.

Philip found a hostel to stay in, in what he decided was a miserable part of town. In his heart, he felt it was the home he'd earned and deserved. By self-will, Philip lingered in Kolkata until the pleading beggars, destitute children, scavengers, and oppressive humidity of the street were as familiar to him as his own pain.

15.

ARYA WAS GLAD to wake up with a destination to go to that morning, because it meant she would be skipping her usual training with Philip. Their last interaction had been hostile and tense, and she wanted some time to pass before seeing him again. She meandered down Sudder Street, treating herself to a warm cup of chai from a local vendor, then strolled toward Chowringhee with the dense atmosphere of the city buzzing around her.

She walked for several minutes and then hailed an autorickshaw to get to school. The driver, smiling with his betel-stained teeth, deftly navigated the city's bustling traffic, expertly dodging cars and walkers. To Arya, the chaos of Kolkata's streets and its reckless drivers, once daunting, now felt like a regular and enjoyable part of her day.

She got there sooner than anticipated, a good fifteen minutes before class was set to begin. Recalling what Sister Maria had said standing outside, her gaze landed on the brothel down the street. A flurry of questions filled her mind. Compelled by a mix of curiosity, she made her way closer to get a firsthand look at the building.

The ground floor had windows that were barred, and heavy tapestries hung behind them. Arya lingered outside, curious about who might enter or leave. After a brief pause, a hand discreetly shifted a section of the drape, unveiling the eyes of a young girl who looked no older than eighteen. Her eyes held a depth of experience, and without speaking, Arya knew how ugly those experiences were because she'd known them too. In a moment of unexpected connection, she saw herself.

Moments later, as Sister Maria briskly walked up the street, she was taken aback to see Arya outside the brothel, in the company of two women. Communication was limited—the women didn't speak English, and Arya was restricted to mere smiles and eye contact. Yet, through those silent exchanges, Arya read the stories in their eyes, and they, in return, recognized compassion and acceptance in hers.

"Arya," Sister Maria's voice broke through, edged with frustration. "Come with me, now."

"Did I do something wrong, Sister?"

"You're putting yourself and these women in danger," Sister Maria said. "I brought you here to volunteer at the school."

"And what about them?" Arya motioned to the women, who watched their conversation with open curiosity.

"Not now!" Sister Maria snapped back. "You are my guest here, and I'm telling you to come with me, or you will create problems with Garu."

The women's immediate tension at the name hinted a dark connection.

"Who's Garu?"

"They work for him."

Arya gave the women one last look before joining Sister Maria. The walk back to the school was quiet, but Arya had a lot of questions, especially about why Sister Maria seemed uneasy about the women from the brothel. For now, she kept them to herself.

Once inside, she went straight to the first-grade classroom to help Sister Catherine. Today, she felt more valuable, as she was the only volunteer around. The kids practiced their English spelling, and Arya moved around, checking their work. Gita and Podip, who she'd spent more time with, did particularly well, getting all their spellings right.

At the first morning break, Sister Maria invited Arya to sit with her on a bench in the courtyard.

"I know you have a good heart," she started, trying to reach an understanding.

"How could you know that?"

"Because you're here. No one comes to Kolkata by mistake. They are drawn here."

"Were you?"

"Yes, dear, I was. And I was like you, full of compassion, but also anger. But I learned, especially as a nun, that not every battle is mine to fight."

For a moment, the two sat quietly, basking in the gentle embrace of the morning sun. The lively shouts and laughter of children echoed around them. Gita and

Podip approached, their hands intertwined, as they joyfully skipped their way over.

"We're gonna be teachers when we grow up!" Gita declared with a grin.

"That's a big job. You have a lot of learning to do," Sister Maria said, smiling.

"They're good at their lessons," Arya added, nodding at the two kids.

"Today we have...science and...um…"

"Geography," Podip said, finishing her sentence.

"You might have to teach me those things," Arya jested.

As the bell rang, signaling the end of recess, Arya followed Gita and Podip back to their classroom. Once inside, Sister Catherine, with Arya's help, unfurled a massive map of India across the front blackboard. They showed the kids where Kolkata was on the map and pointed out the big Bay of Bengal. Then, Sister Catherine taught them about the Himalayas, and how the mountains sent cold winds that inevitably brought the monsoon rains. In science class, Gita and Podip learned about the cycle of water, how rain comes from clouds and how water, after falling on the ground, evaporated back up to the sky.

At the end of the day, Arya exited the school building amidst a sea of children, all eager to step out into the sunlit courtyard. From the corner of her eye, she spotted a figure lingering behind the green gate, partially hidden by its panels. It was a woman, standing somewhat hesitantly. Recognizing her, Sister Maria swiftly made her way over. She unhitched the latch and swung the gate open, revealing Bimala, who had come from down the street for a visit with her son, Podip.

"Mama!" Podip shouted, spotting her across the courtyard. He bolted towards her and leaped into her embrace, his face nestled against her sari.

Arya's gaze settled on Bimala, recognizing the distinctive yellow sari she wore. A flashback from several weeks ago surfaced in her mind–Bimala being hassled by two men on the street. Now, as Bimala held Podip tight, her eyes flicked with unease toward the gate. For a brief moment, she raised her gaze to Arya, offering a solemn look of gratitude in silent acknowledgment of what she did.

Podip pulled at Bimala's sari, looking to regain her attention. "Mama, I did good today," he said in Bengali, looking for her approval.

"Good for you." She smiled.

"I got perfect marks today." Podip begged of his mother, Bimala, speaking in Bengali, tugging on her sari to regain her attention.

"Good for you!" Bimala said.

"Want to see?" Podip's finger pointed towards the school door.

Just then, Gita approached, her eyes searching Bimala's face. "Have you seen my mother?"

"I'm sorry, Podip. Not today. And Gita, I haven't seen her," Bimala replied gently.

A shadow of disappointment crossed Gita's face.

"He waits for you," she whispered, nodding towards Podip.

After a few quiet moments, Bimala planted a kiss on the top of her son's head and stood. She ran her hand over her sari to iron out the wrinkles and then made her way to the gate. Podip watched her leave with a heavy heart.

The scene with Bimala and Podip left a heavy mark on Arya, and it weighed on her during the trip back to the hostel.

That night, she made her way to the rooftop. Philip was there, beer in one hand, cigarette in the other, staring out at the city. His boots kicked up lazily on the railing. Arya approached, wary of the mood.

"We good?"

Philip took a drag, exhaling slowly before replying. "Yeah, we're good."

"What's on your mind?" she asked, moving a bit closer to him.

"You got me thinking. Maybe there's a way to make some money here. The underground boxing club I mentioned to you. There's live betting there."

"I thought you said women can't fight."

"You wouldn't be fighting. We'll size up the fighters, play the odds, and bet money to make money."

"I want to see this place. When can we go?"

He paused for a moment, the dim light reflecting off his glass. "Next fight is set for tomorrow night," he replied, taking a final sip from his beer and setting it down.

Arya tried to imagine for a moment what an underground boxing venue in Kolkata might be like.

"Come on, let's get started."

She gave a brief nod, then reached for the jump rope, quickly falling into a steady rhythm. After she finished, Philip stepped in with the pads, setting the pace for a demanding session, words were seldom exchanged during training. At the end, Arya retreated to her room, fatigued in her muscles, but with a growing sense of anticipation about the upcoming visit to the venue.

The next evening, Philip knocked on her door, ready to go. They descended to the street and caught a taxi, setting off for the Rajarhat district, forty-five minutes away.

As the taxi rolled to a stop, Arya's gaze swept over the unruly lineup of cars that filled the sprawling lot, leading up to a modest one-story building. The muffled roars and chatter from within pierced the silence outside, hinting at the energy and intensity inside.

"Walk past them. Don't make eye contact," Philip whispered, guiding her swiftly past the bouncers at the door and into the building.

The room was dense with tension and chatter. They pushed their way through, standing behind a group of onlookers. All eyes, including theirs, were fixed on the two fighters in the ring, throwing punches in a no-nonsense battle.

"See. I'd put my money on the short guy. He doesn't have the height advantage, but he moves right. He slips in without getting hit. I'd bet people in this crowd won't see it that way. They'll favor the bigger man," Philip said, explaining his strategy to win at gambling.

The shorter fighter ducked, narrowly missing a left hook, then sprang up with a sudden uppercut, stunning his opponent before the end of the round.

Arya took a moment to survey her surroundings, absorbing the unexpected scene. In a city as diverse as Kolkata, where contrasts of affluence and need were evident, she was grateful for boxing. She noted the crowd was unlike any she'd encountered in her time in India. A mix of wealthy Indians and foreigners, well-dressed and in pursuit of illicit thrills.

After the minute break, the bell rang, and the fighters returned to the center of the ring. The taller guy seemed dominant initially, but Philip's pick, the shorter one, landed a powerful combo. A sharp body shot followed by a right that sent the opponent's mouthguard flying. The crowd went wild.

"That's what I'm talking about."

"So, how do we get in on this?"

"Next time. We'll approach him," Philip said, gesturing toward a man on the other side of the ring. "That's Garu. He's the main guy here." Following Philip's finger, Arya looked and spotted Garu sitting at a table, surrounded by his men.

"Garu?" she repeated.

16.

SISTER MARIA HELD her rosary, gently moving the beads along the string as she whispered prayers in the early morning sun. Beside her, Arya sat in quiet contemplation, her attention on Gita and Podip climbing to the top of the jungle gym to take turns swinging from the monkey bars. Sensing something in her periphery, she turned her head towards the gate. Arya squinted to see through the gaps in the paneling, barely discerning the outline of a young girl.

Yunni stood there, her eyes filled with longing as she watched the boys and girls play, yearning for the stolen moments of her own childhood. Arya nudged Sister Maria to look. In that moment, Bimala appeared behind the green gate. She took Yunni by the arm, leading her away, back up the street.

"What was that, Sister?"

"I will ask Bimala about it when I speak with her next," Sister Maria replied.

Disturbed by the heartbreaking reality of a child at the brothel, not uncommon in Kolkata, Arya searched Sister Maria's eyes for answers about how to feel about such injustice. Where she expected anger, Arya saw only compassion.

As the bell rang, signaling the first period, the children and teachers filed into the school building, and Arya followed along. In the classroom, assisting Sister

Catherine, her thoughts repeatedly returned to the young girl outside the gate. The image of that child weighed heavily on her mind and raised questions about her own future in Kolkata. She was determined to ensure her continued stay, and couldn't help but consider betting on underground fights that Philip had suggested to make some quick cash.

• • •

That evening, in a brothel room that smelled like body odor and sandalwood incense, Bimala dressed Yunni in a rose-colored sari and painted her face with bright makeup. Soon, Garu would begin showing her to high-paying customers, and he needed his virgin ready for the bidding process. Hot tears streamed from Yunni's eyes, catching the mascara, dripping black down her young cheeks.

"Please, I want to go home."

"Don't cry, it will ruin your face!" Bimala said, shaking the girl by the shoulders. "He expects a very high price for you."

The words made Yunni cry more because she feared never seeing her family again, unaware they were the ones who had sold her like a goat.

"Trust me, there are worse places," Bimala pleaded with the girl, beginning to work the knots out of her long black hair with her purple brush. "Here you will wear nice clothes, and you will have food every night, and a bed to sleep."

Yunni sobbed, trembling in her new silk sari. Seeing the girl in such despair, Bimala abandoned the brush and embraced her tightly. She thought of Podip and what lay ahead for him. In a sudden surge of bravery and defiance, Bimala retrieved a handful of rupees from her blouse, and placed them in the girl's hand. *Om Krim Kalikaye Namaha,* she prayed silently before speaking as a mother.

"Can you find your way home?"

"I came here on a train...it can take me back?"

"Yes. I will show you how to get to the station. Tell the man at the ticket booth the name of your village in Bangladesh. He will tell you which train." Bimala tiptoed out of the room, peering down the hallway. With no one in sight from the top of the stairs, she quietly snuck Yunni outside and took her around the corner. "Take a taxi to Chitpur Station. Go!" she said, pointing her down the street.

Yunni gave her a desperately grateful look and hurriedly dashed down the street. Bimala watched until the girl disappeared in the distance, then returned inside. In her mind, she began to craft the narrative she would share with the other women, detailing how Yunni had escaped and fled during the middle of the night.

Unbeknownst to Bimala, one of the other girls in the brothel had witnessed the betrayal from across the street, standing in plain sight. She immediately dialed Sandeep, who in turn called Garu.

"We have a problem, sir."

"What is it?" Garu asked, answering from his couch at home.

"The girl, Yunni, escaped."

"How?"

"Bimala."

"Stupid whore!" Garu shouted, pounding on the coffee table. "Find her quickly!"

Hanging up the phone, Garu leaned back, slipped a piece of opium under his tongue, and lit a cigarette. Above all, he despised losing money. He took a deep drag and exhaled slowly, letting the smoke waft over his neatly pruned mustache. Regardless of whether Yunni turned up, he had faith in his man's ability to instill fear. He made an example of traitors.

Sandeep swiftly made his way to Bhowanipore, where he had a short conversation with Bimala. Without wasting a moment, he rushed to Chitpur station. Amidst the bustling crowds, he diligently searched the departure hall and the train platforms. It didn't take long before he spotted Yunni hiding in a dimly lit corner, anxiously waiting for the Dhaka train to depart.

The next morning, Garu returned to his jewelry store to find Sandeep waiting with Yunni by his side. Fresh tears streaked down the young girl's face, and she still wore the same silk sari Bimala had dressed her in the night before, fabric soiled and torn.

"You won't be a poor investment for me, little one," Garu said, settling behind his desk. Opening the top drawer, he retrieved a small silver cosmetics box, removed the lid, and gently tapped the side, causing some of the brown powder to cascade onto his desk. He then pulled a credit card from his wallet and began to straighten the powder into a line.

"Give her!" Garu shouted.

Sandeep seized the back of Yunni's neck, his grip unyielding, and forced her face down onto the desk. With a single, powerful motion, he maneuvered her into position.

"Sniff it!" he barked, his voice commanding and harsh, as he continued to push her face down.

Terrified and desperate, Yunni complied, inhaling sharply through her nose, drawing the powder up into her nostrils.

A few moments later, Sandeep felt her small muscles relaxing in his grip. When she stopped squirming, he released her, and she stood with her eyes closed, nearly keeling over from the sedation.

"Four days, you will give her," Garu said, handing Sandeep the silver box.

"Then take her back to Bhowanipore. She will not leave again."

Using drugs as a means to maintain control over his girls, Garu knew once they were addicted, it would become nearly impossible for them to leave. He reserved this tactic with the ones who resisted authority, but as their bodies became accustomed, he would have their obedience and sell them many times over.

...

The following morning, just as daylight began to seep through the horizon, Sister Maria stood by the green gate, eyes fixed on the paramedics as they carefully loaded a lifeless figure, concealed beneath a white sheet, into their waiting ambulance. It was at this moment that Dhriti appeared on the other side of the gate, locking eyes with Sister Maria and uttering a single name.

"Bimala."

Without another word, Dhriti quietly retreated down the bustling street, while the ambulance disappeared into morning traffic. Sister Maria inhaled deeply, trying to fathom the gravity of what she had just learned. Today, she faced the task of conveying the most devastating news imaginable to a six-year-old boy—the loss of his mother.

Podip was engrossed in playing with Gita on the jungle gym. Sister Maria approached them, and as the bell rang, signifying the start of the school day, she requested their presence on the ground.

"Podip, there is something I must tell you."

Gita chose to stay with her friend. As the other classes began to make their way into the building, Sister Catherine sensed that something was amiss and held back the first-grade class. Unfortunately, it was precisely at this moment that Arya arrived, with Philip reluctantly in tow. Having been persuaded, he came to see her work with the nuns—on the most inopportune day.

Sister Maria knelt before Podip, her voice soft and filled with sorrow, as she gently conveyed the news. Gita stood nearby, her face devoid of emotion, while Podip began to sob hysterically, burying his face in Sister Maria's sari.

"What's going on?" Arya asked, rushing over.

"Auntie Bimala passed last night," Sister Maria whispered softly.

"Mama's dead," Podip screamed, lifting his wet face from the damp sari.

Jun and Hiro observed the scene from the doorway of the school building, standing at a distance as the cries of "Mama! I want Mama!" echoed through the courtyard.

His classmates gathered, forming a tight circle around him. Sister Maria continued to cradle Podip in her arms, offering comfort until his sobs began to subside. After a few moments, she turned to Sister Catherine and gently requested that she guide Podip to the dormitory, where he could find some solace and, perhaps, take a nap. Gita followed them, her young face bearing a solemn expression that seemed out of place for a child her age.

As they walked away, Arya approached Sister Maria. "What happened?" she inquired.

Sister Maria, surprised to see Philip there on such an unfortunate day, gestured for Arya to follow her. She led them away from the children, heading towards the gate and stopping about fifty feet from the school building. "One of the women told me that it was Bimala."

"How did she die?" Arya pressed for more information.

"We don't know yet," Sister Maria replied, her voice echoing sadness.

"We should speak to Garu," Arya suggested.

"Garu?" Philip asked, looking at Arya with confusion. *It can't be the same guy.*

"I do not speak with him," Sister Maria replied, her expression growing more serious. "Our job is to protect the children."

"I'll talk to him," Arya insisted.

Sister Maria shook her head, concern etched on her face. "I brought Gita and Podip to this school. I know better than you how dangerous Garu is."

"Someone killed Podip's mother!" Arya shouted, her emotions taking over. To stop herself from saying more, she stormed out of the school, leaving them in an awkward silence.

Sister Maria studied Philip with renewed interest. "Why did you come today?"

"She wanted to show me the work she does with you," Philip explained.

"And you're her coach—"

"Isn't that what you said to do? Help someone? She's a fighter..."

"Some fighters lose and never get back up," Sister Maria said solemnly, placing a hand on Philip's shoulder. "Don't let that happen to her, Philip. Please."

17.

UNABLE TO CONTAIN her anger, Arya took an autorickshaw back to the hostel. Once in her room, she began to strike the wall with her fists, feeling an overwhelming surge of emotions for Bimala and Podip. Seated at the edge of her bed, she could hardly believe this was real. *They killed her, got rid of her like trash.* The injustice gnawed at her.

Since Terrance's demise, Arya had been moving through life with an unshakable sense of being a lone survivor. The thought echoed within her and had served as the motivator, pushing her to break free from addiction. Bimala's tragic death served as a stark reminder that she was not alone in her suffering, and it sent a shiver down Arya's spine. After witnessing the suffering at Nirmal Hriday, and the joy at Karuna Dan, Arya felt the sincere desire to be *good*, and for the first time in her life, dared to believe it was possible. In Bimala, she also saw herself, and it stirred up her darkest feelings. Rather than turning inward, Arya channeled her emotions into a singular target for her outrage. Garu.

As her mood darkened further, Arya began to think about getting high. That familiar irritability, just beneath the skin, resurfaced. She paced restlessly between her bed and the door, searching for a way to quell the noise without heroin.

In the early afternoon, Arya stepped out of the hostel and made her way to a bar on Sudder Street. It presented itself as an ordinary establishment, resembling more of a restaurant than a pub. Inside, a dozen patrons, a mix of locals and foreigners, sat hunched over pints of pale ale. Arya ordered a whiskey in an attempt to calm her frayed nerves and found an empty table to occupy.

As the patrons around her remained engrossed in their own worlds, Arya sought solace in a second and then a third drink. The alcohol loosened the tension in her shoulders, granting her deeper breaths and a measure of relief from the stress. But the buzz was bittersweet because she knew there were harder drugs nearby. Determined to resist a full on relapse, Arya continued to drink. By the time Jun and Hiro came coincidentally walking through the door, she was already steeped in liquor.

They joined her at the table as the sun began its descent outside. Although neither Jun nor Hiro mentioned Bimala, the somber atmosphere and their subdued demeanor indicated that the news of Podip's mother had affected them as well.

"You're drinking today..." Jun remarked, seeing Arya consume alcohol for the first time.

"Today, I am," she replied.

Jun signaled the bartender for two beers and another whiskey for Arya. As the evening unfolded, he and Hiro resorted to conversing in Japanese, a welcome relief for Arya, who had little desire to talk. She drank in silence as the hours slipped away, boiling with anger at Philip for his selfishness, Sister Maria for her perceived cowardice, and Garu, for representing everything she hated in this world.

When Jun and Hiro decided it was time to go, they glanced at Arya and clearly saw how drunk she was. "We're heading back. Come with us," Jun said, extending his hand in a friendly manner.

"No thanks," Arya slurred, swatting his hand away.

"You've had a lot to drink. Please, come home," Jun urged.

"Don't call it home…with that asshole on the roof…" Arya mumbled.

Jun and Hiro exchanged sympathetic glances before quietly leaving.

Arya, too drunk and aggravated to concern herself with the disapproving looks she received, finished the last of her whiskey before making her way to the exit. She didn't head back to the hostel; instead, she walked out onto Chowringhee and hailed an autorickshaw. Though her stated destination was the school, her true plan was to disembark further down the street.

Dim light filtered through drawn tapestries, casting a faint glow on the quiet street. The few pedestrians who ventured out this late kept to themselves, their presence barely noticed. From behind the tapestry, Dhriti spotted Arya and promptly called Sandeep. As it happened, Sandeep was with Garu, just around the corner.

Arya watched as the chauffeured car pulled up, and Sandeep, accompanied by Nurul, exited from the back doors and made their way toward her.

"Chalo!" Sandeep called out to Arya, approaching her at the entrance. "Leave!" he repeated in English.

Unsteady on her feet, Arya reached for her cellphone, activated the camera, and pointed it at them. She swept the camera across the vehicle, capturing the license plates and the brothel building before returning her gaze to them.

"I want to speak with Garu," she asserted firmly.

"Garu's not here. Leave!" Sandeep barked in response.

"Turn it off!" Nurul chimed in, pointing at Arya's phone.

Sandeep walked over to the black car and tapped on the roof three times. The front passenger window glided down, and he engaged in a brief exchange in Bengali through the gap. Then suddenly, the car door swung open, and Garu emerged onto the street. He walked toward Arya without hesitation, unconcerned by the presence of her camera.

"What do you want?"

"Tell me about Bimala," she demanded.

"I don't know who Bimala is," he said, casting a quick glance at Sandeep before returning his gaze to Arya. "You're just a tourist. Go home."

"I'll stay right here. I'm going to show the world what pieces of shit you are," she declared, exhaling whiskey fumes into the air.

"Stupid whore!" Garu responded with a brutal slap that sent her head spinning. Arya lost her grip on the phone, and it fell, skidding across the pavement. From behind, Sandeep and Nurul swiftly moved in, restraining her by pinning her arms behind her back. Seizing the opportunity, Garu slammed Arya in the gut, causing her to gasp for air. He followed it with another harsh slap across her face. When Sandeep and Nurul finally released her, she crumpled to the ground, struggling to breathe.

As she scrambled to get back on her feet, Sandeep swiftly struck her on the side of the head, knocking her down again. She watched Garu stomping on her phone, his heel coming down repeatedly on the cracked screen. "Teach her a lesson," he commanded, returning to his car.

Instantly, Sandeep and Nurul unleashed a barrage of kicks upon Arya. She cowered, doing her best to shield herself from the onslaught. Arya tucked her head and elbows in, absorbing the relentless blows on her ribs and shoulders. The searing pain from each kick left her convinced that her bones were breaking. In less than a minute, the brutal assault came to an abrupt halt as Sandeep retrieved a switchblade from his pocket. He leaned over Arya, intending to scar her face as a permanent reminder to never utter Garu's name again.

A woman's voice shattered the tension. "Hey! Stop! Hey, you! Stop!"

Sandeep looked up and saw a nun dressed in white rushing toward him, accompanied by two Asian men. It was Sister Maria, who, after hearing from Jun and Hiro about Arya's drunken state at the bar, had brought them here on intuition.

Sandeep quickly withdrew the blade, took a step back, and exchanged glances with Nurul. Startled by three individuals coming to Arya's aid, they swiftly turned and sprinted in the opposite direction until they were out of sight.

Sister Maria knelt beside Arya, her face filled with concern, and examined her body for signs of severe injury. "Let me check if something is broken," she said, gently running her hands over her.

"I'm okay," Arya said, her voice weak but reassuring.

Working together, Sister Maria, Jun, and Hiro helped Arya to her feet and guided her into the back seat of a taxi, headed back to the hostel.

18.

AFTER PATCHING ARYA up, Sister Maria and Jun stayed to make sure she was okay. Arya was quiet, her head throbbing from the start of a brutal hangover. She avoided looking into their eyes. There were cuts on her face, arms, and legs, and an icepack pressed against her bruised ribs. The room was silent except for the occasional rustle of the bedsheets . Suddenly, the door swung open. Philip had heard from Babu about Arya's condition.

"What the fuck have you done?" His voice cut through the room, its intensity startling both Sister Maria and Jun. Arya's face went pale as she looked up at him.

"She's okay, no broken bones," Sister Maria interjected, hoping to calm the situation.

"I found out some things about Garu. It's the same guy from the boxing club. He's a gangster. He could have killed you."

"I know…" Arya murmured, sitting up in bed.

"You're a joke," Philip scoffed. "You have no idea what you're doing and no idea who you're messing with."

"Fuck you!" Arya exploded, reacting to the insult.

"Enough!" Sister Maria interjected sharply, her patience worn thin. As silence settled in the room, Jun quietly slipped out, sensing it was time to give them space.

"I'd like to be alone please," Arya whispered as she sat up in bed, fresh tears dripping onto the sheets. Philip obliged and walked out at once, leaving her alone with Sister Maria.

"Why did you do it?" she probed.

"I hate myself," Arya admitted, continuing to cry. "I wish I could be like you. Good. Kind."

"You are," Sister Maria responded with a smile. "But you have to stop fighting with yourself, Arya. I learned that years ago."

"How?"

"By coming to Kolkata," she replied, looking up at the vibrant painting of Kali that Arya had put up on the wall. "Take the weekend to rest. We'll talk more next week if you feel comfortable coming back to Karuna Dan." Sister Maria then quietly left.

Arya wrapped herself in her covers, trying to escape into sleep, but memories of faceless strangers and drug-fueled nights from the not-so-distant past tormented her mind. Her run-in with Garu wasn't just a mistake—it seemed a reflection of all the things she hadn't yet faced. After what felt like hours of wrestling with her memories, like a relentless throbbing in her head, exhaustion finally overtook her, and she succumbed to a restless sleep.

She awoke the next morning, unrested, irritable, and quite hungover. She put on her sunglasses and walked out of the hostel, headed straight for one of the chai stands. Two cups to wake up and she bought a pack of cigarettes, smoking them one after the other as she walked. The air was thick, and she bumped elbows with pedestrians as she navigated her way through the crowds. As beggar women with babies called out, "Ma! Ma! Ma!" and tried to touch her, rubbing their palms on her clothes to get her attention. She kept walking, unmoved, eyes blank, numb to the world around her.

Casually wandering down Chowringhee, Arya laid eyes on the row of yellow taxis parked near the sidewalk and immediately noticed him there. He was smoking next to his car, offering her a grin of stained teeth because he remembered her from several weeks ago. An intense craving for heroin started to rise within her. Her mind tempted her with promises of relief from the pain and shame she carried, even if just temporarily. The yearning for it was overwhelming.

Her stomach turned in anticipation, and her skin erupted in goosebumps, as if her body already knew what was coming. She took a step closer to him and met his murky yellow eyes in a shared, silent understanding.

"What you want?" he inquired, his tone tinged with a hint of impatience from having wasted his effort the last time she'd come around.

"Brown sugar," she said clearly, her gaze locked on his, showing her seriousness.

The taxi driver signaled to the young boy working with the parking attendants with a casual wave, calling him forth to look after his car while he went on a short trip. He proceeded down one of the side streets, and Arya followed him through the labyrinth, retracing the very same path they had ventured before. They arrived at the doorstep of the crumbling building, its facade hanging over a dimly lit lobby.

The driver's gravelly voice broke the stillness as he summoned the one-armed man, who appeared a few seconds later like a ghost out of the shadows. He was just as unsettling as before, with one arm, thin and weathered from decades of intravenous drug use. The taxi driver turned to Arya, looking to make a fee in the exchange.

"What you want?" he repeated.

"How much for this?" Arya asked, reaching into her pocket to reveal a wad of rupees.

She knew it was more than enough to secure a substantial bag of heroin, considering she was doing the math with New York prices. She counted the money right in front of them, and the one-armed man retrieved four neatly wrapped grams from his pocket and handed them over to the taxi driver, who, in turn, passed them to her. Arya accepted them without a word, her intent clear and turned to leave.

On the way back to the hostel, she stopped in a pharmacy and bought a handful of syringes. If she was going to relapse, she'd have to take it all the way.

• • •

In the apartment above Garu's jewelry store, Yunni resisted Sandeep each time he tried to give her heroin, but after a few days, her will to fight had faded. He continued giving her the drug, watching as her fragile young body became increasingly dependent. Only after a week had passed, and Yunni was devoid of any signs of the scared and rebellious child they'd seen, Garu declared it was time to bring her back to the brothel. They placed her in a car headed for Bhowanipore, where she arrived late in the afternoon. As they entered, Yunni wore a vacant, hollow look in her eyes. Her movements were sluggish and lethargic, weighed down by the chemicals in her blood.

Garu firmly grasped her shoulders and guided her down the dimly lit hallway towards a room on the first floor where another one of his investments awaited. Dhriti, at only twenty years old, didn't boast the same beauty as Bimala, but her awareness of who held the reins was evident. She had alerted Sandeep when Yunni had tried to escape and informed him of Arya's presence lurking outside that night. However, after witnessing the outcomes of her actions, the virtue of that loyalty was in question.

"Prepare her for work," Garu commanded sternly. "And expect Sandeep to visit her at least once a day."

"Yes, sir," Dhriti replied nervously. She adjusted her sari and stepped forward, gently taking Yunni by the hand.

"Do not disappoint me," Garu warned before leaving them alone.

As Dhriti closed the door to the room, she couldn't help but wonder if Yunni would attempt another escape. However, the girl standing before her was no longer the same despondent soul from before, filled with tears and hope for freedom. This time, Yunni's spirit was drained to a point where escape seemed all but impossible. Word quickly spread down the hallway that Yunni had returned, causing the other women to maintain a cautious distance to avoid incurring Garu's wrath.

Garu and Sandeep made their way to the boxing club in Rajarhat to meet the two constables, now officially on the payroll, before the spectators arrived. This night marked the officers' first time overseeing security for the venue, and Garu wanted to ensure they were fully prepared for the responsibility. He also had some matters to discuss with Rakesh, the owner of the Balaji Boxing Gym.

Upon their early arrival, they found the final training session still underway, featuring a dozen young women with wrists carefully wrapped, diligently practicing their boxing techniques. Dressed in a green tracksuit with white stripes, Rakesh paced before the group, guiding them through various combinations, offering detailed explanations on the mechanics of good form.

"When you throw the jab, the right covers here," he said, holding his left arm out, covering the right eye with his opposite hand. "To throw a right, you must shift your weight to the other side." He demonstrated each punch, emphasizing rotation of the hips.

The girls hung on his every word, not just because he was their coach, but also a former national champion with a remarkable record of forty professional fights. Rakesh had initially set out to train male fighters. He came to see it was the young women aged fifteen to eighteen who displayed the greatest potential.

Right then, two girls arrived very late, at the tail end of the session. They frantically rushed to wrap their hands and join the ongoing class. Noticing them come in, Rakesh also saw Garu at the door, and made a conscious effort to conceal the disdain on his face. Renting out the gym to Garu was a deep source of pain for Rakesh, who did it for the money. Most of his students were poor, and the fees he charged them were hardly enough to keep the lights on.

"I know many of you share your gloves and equipment, and do not have the money to afford even a proper diet," he said, providing some words of encouragement to the class. "Some of you do not even have the bus fare to come… but it does not matter. In the ring, it does not matter if you are Hindu, or Muslim, or Sikh. It does not matter whether you are rich or poor. Kolkata is the home of Indian boxing, and you are part of that tradition. Do you hear me?"

"Yes, sir!" the girls shouted in unison.

"Finish on the heavy bags! Go!" Rakesh said, releasing his students to the other side of the hall so he could reluctantly greet Garu and his men. The young women dashed to the opposite end of the gym where the heavy bags dangled from the scaffolded beams.

"You're early," Rakesh said, approaching with measured steps.

"Tonight, we expect more people and more money, so we will have police protection," Garu said, smiling. "A lot of money is being gambled on these fights…that's why I pay to use your shitty gym."

Rakesh maintained his silence, prioritizing his students over his wounded pride. Outside, trucks arrived carrying chairs and refreshments for the evening's event. Garu, Sandeep, and Nurul attended to the logistics, overseeing the placement of chairs, tables, and coolers around the hall, leaving Rakesh to complete his final session and ensure his students left the premises before the influx of fight fans.

As Sandeep and Nurul directed the workers in setting up, Garu walked with the two constables, indicating his designated seat and the location of the money. He strategically positioned them a row behind him, providing them with a clear view of any potential threats and ample time to react if necessary.

With his table arranged to his satisfaction, Garu cracked open a fresh bottle of scotch and motioned for Sandeep to join him. Just as the first spectators began to trickle in, Garu leaned in and gestured toward the ring.

"What do you think?" he asked, his gaze fixed on the ring.

"I'm ready," Sandeep replied.

"Then I'll arrange a fight for you soon," Garu affirmed, sliding a glass of whiskey across the table. "Win for me, and I'll make you rich."

19.

ARYA REMAINED SELF-CONFINED in her room for three days, getting high, refusing to answer Sister Maria's persistent knocks and calls through the door. Philip's voice hadn't come through the door to scold her, for which she was glad. The only person she did answer was Chaiwallah, since he brought provisions—food, water, and cigarettes—that she needed to keep up her isolation.

The heroin wasn't quite as strong as what she was used to in New York. She compulsively injected herself multiple times, chasing a high just out of reach, leaving fresh track marks along her arms. *How am I supposed to go back to the school looking like this?* she thought, looking down at the wounds across her skin. She wasn't sure Sister Maria would allow her to come back, having caused a scene down the street from the school, potentially endangering the children.

Sister Maria had trusted her to come to Nirmal Hriday and then Karuna Dan to work with Gita and Podip. Philip had agreed to be her coach and gave his time, and she'd let them both down. Reflecting on the fortuitous nature of her journey—finding the money in Terrance's apartment to volunteering with the missionaries—Arya questioned if she'd squandered her one chance.

Sequestered in her room in a state she did not wish to show the world, Arya reached for her lighter and spoon. She fixed herself a heavy shot, the liquid in the syringe a dark brown. Finding a vein, she pushed it into her bloodstream and let her eyes close one more time.

As evening descended, Philip and Sister Maria, concerned over her prolonged absence, approached the door together having already confirmed with Babu and Chaiwallah that she was still residing at the hostel. Sister Maria rapped sharply three times.

"Arya?" she called out, the urgency evident in her voice.

The silence that followed lasted too long.

"Arya, please. We're concerned," she persisted, knocking more forcefully. Receiving no answer, she turned to Philip. "Please, you try."

He banged on the door several times, rattling the door in its frame. "Come on, Arya... Open it! There ain't much point hiding in there. Don't make me knock this door down!" He paused for a second, questioning if he truly wished to be involved.

"Break it!" Sister Maria cried out.

Taking a few steps back, Philip kicked in the door, ripping the padlock anchor free. The sight before them was chilling. Arya was sprawled on the bed, scars vivid on her pale arm as it dangled over the edge. With her eyes closed and lips tinged blue, chest still, showing no signs of breathing, she appeared to be dead.

Sister Maria rushed to Arya's side, gripping her shoulders in a desperate attempt to shake her awake.

Used needles and empty drug bags were scattered on the bed.

"Arya! Do you hear me?" she shouted, Arya's body heavy in her hands. "She has a pulse—"

"She's overdosed, Sister. We need an ambulance," Philip said, rushing to make the call.

Desperately, Sister Maria slapped Arya's leg, shouting her name, trying to rouse her from her unconscious state. By the time the distant sound of ambulance sirens grew louder, Babu, Chaiwallah, and several hostel guests, alerted by the commotion, had emerged to see what was happening. Two paramedics rushed into the hostel, swiftly securing Arya onto a stretcher and loading her into the waiting ambulance. Sister Maria and Philip trailed in a taxi.

In a private room at the hospital, Arya rested, unaware that Sister Maria and Philip were waiting just outside under the bright fluorescent lights. A young doctor named Dr. Gosh came up, informing them that the paramedics had managed to reverse Arya's overdose en route, using a medication that cleared the heroin from her system. This abrupt reversal thrust her into immediate opioid withdrawal. To mitigate her distress and curb her combative response to the sudden withdrawal, the medical team administered a sedative, rendering her unconscious for the remainder of the night.

"We've stabilized her. If you hadn't brought her in, she might not have made it. You should look at getting her into an addiction treatment program, but we will release her in the morning."

"Are you fucking serious?" Philip shouted. "She'll go right back!"

"We're not equipped to handle addiction. This bed is for someone in critical condition," Dr. Gosh said dispassionately. "There are sick people who need the bed more than your—"

"Thank you, Doctor," Sister Maria interrupted, cutting the doctor off abruptly, giving him permission to leave. Dr. Gosh nodded politely and retreated back down the hallway.

"She's going to die, you know," Philip said, anger evident in his eyes.

"Both of you need a reason to hold on, Philip. Let's go back and prepare for her return."

Philip saw Sister Maria home that night, and the following dawn, they cleaned out Arya's room, discarding any remnants of drugs. By the time they reached the hospital, Arya was dressed and waiting. She seemed pale and gaunt. She wouldn't meet their eyes. In the taxi, she remained quiet, her gaze anchored to the floor.

When they reached the hostel, she walked with them, her steps heavy, and only spoke once they were inside her room.

"I know you saved my life. I don't know how to thank you for something like that. I can't tell you why I did it," Arya said in a low voice laden with guilt. "I'm sorry—"

"You're sorry? For nearly killing yourself?" Philip cut in, his voice rising in frustration, compounding her shame.

Sister Maria gently placed her rosary on the table beside her and moved closer to Arya. "I believe God has brought you here for a reason."

Arya's eyes lifted, catching a hint of encouragement in the unexpected words.

"You're not bloody proselytizing, are you, Sister? This ain't the time for religion. She just overdosed on heroin."

"She needs something to fight for, and so do you," Sister Maria said. "We are here because you wanted to speak with Garu," she said, speaking to Arya. "What did you accomplish?"

"Nothing."

"I learned from one of the brothel women that Garu has a girl there. Twelve or thirteen. The one we saw outside the gate. Bimala tried to help her escape."

"Christ..." Philip exhaled sharply, giving Sister Maria a reproachful look. "She doesn't need more problems, especially not yours." Beneath his anger, Arya saw raw vulnerability in his concern for her.

"And I understand the power of faith," she replied evenly, glancing at the picture of the deity hanging a few feet from Arya. "It can guide us even through our darkest times."

She reached into her sari and pulled out a piece of paper. She unfolded it and showed it to them. It appeared to be a page ripped from a book. The excerpt was about Kolkata and featured a color representation of Kali, taking up nearly a third of the page. It was the same goddess as the one on the wall, with black skin, four arms, and a necklace of skulls around her neck. A long tongue hung out of her mouth, dripping blood. Arya was reminded of her father and wondered what meaning the deity had held for him.

"God doesn't just live in the nice places... As a Christian, you can imagine, revering her is not something that is easily understood, but Kolkata is the city of Kali. When I think of her, I also think of you," Sister Maria said, speaking directly to Arya. "Tomorrow is the start of the Kali Puja festival. For several days, people in the city will be praying and asking for miracles. I suggest you do the same."

She folded the page with Kali's image, tucked it back into her sari, then gracefully exited the room, leaving a thick silence behind her.

After a while, she turned to Phillip. "Will you still train me?"

"Sure. If it keeps you from killing yourself."

20.

KOLKATA WAS A vibrant symphony of colors and sounds as the city celebrated the auspicious days of Durga Puja—the most important and widely celebrated of Hindu festivals. In a casual conversation between two volunteers, Arya overheard that Durga had defeated a demon, and that she and Kali were revered embodiments of Shakti, a divine feminine energy. On the night of the new moon in the Hindu month of Kartik, Kali sects performed Kali Puja alongside Durga Puja, praying to the fiercer form of the goddess for ultimate transcendence.

For three days, Arya wandered the city, taking in the vibrant sights. The streets buzzed with cultural extravaganzas, showcasing art, music, idol processions, and rituals. These were performed at temporary installations set up by worshippers in every neighborhood. The city came alive as people celebrated the victory of good over evil. Arya was grateful for the distraction. She took a break from volunteering during the festival, giving herself time to reflect and, at Sister Maria's suggestion, pray for miracles.

On the last day of Durga Puja, Arya took a rickshaw to the city's renowned Kali temple, a short distance from her location on Sudder Street. The temple, situated on the banks of the Hooghly River, anchored a vast plaza and was adorned with striking red, white, and black marble slabs. Ornate spires extended from the domed roof, adding a mystical aura. Around the plaza, vendors sold chai, bottled water, and potpourri, catering to visitors and pilgrims seeking refreshment in the midday heat.

Arya navigated through the throngs of pilgrims. Some performed rituals on the spot, chanting and burning incense. Others brought offerings to the Kali statue—rice, lentils, fruits, and baskets filled with fresh hibiscus petals. She ascended the wide stairs leading to the temple's inner sanctum, passing an elderly man deep in meditation. He bore a vermillion mark on his forehead and wore only a white dhoti, his lean chest exposed. He chanted with fervent devotion.

"Om Klim Kalikayei Namaha! Om Klim Kalikayei Namaha! Om Klim Kalikayei Namaha!"

Reaching the top, Arya beheld the Kali statue, carved from black stone and adorned with garlands of marigold. The room was fragrant with sandalwood and jasmine. The idol held a sword and wore a crown, symbolizing her dual role as mother and warrior. As Arya descended, the air was thick with the harmonized chants of arriving pilgrims.

That evening, at the hostel, she trained. Although Philip had braced for a decline in her skills, Arya's focus and energy had improved. She struck the pads with accuracy and finesse, displaying a form Philip hadn't seen from her before, and it was surprising, especially after her relapse.

Arya returned to the school the next day, and Sister Maria welcomed her during the usual volunteering hours. Sister Catherine, Jun, and Hiro were delighted to see her, none of them sharing hurtful glances or remarks. Arya was equally pleased to reunite with Gita and Podip, although their spirits remained low. Podip was now weary and withdrawn, his words barely audible. Gita, having already endured the loss of a mother, vicariously relived her grief. Sister Maria made no mention of the brothel, and Arya steered clear of the green gate during her shift.

"It's good to see you back," Sister Maria remarked, as Arya left at the end of the school day.

"Thank you," Arya replied, appreciating the trust and dignity extended to her.

Later, during her session, Arya's sharpness and intensity from the previous night persisted. Impressed by this newfound energy, Philip pushed her to the limit, until they were both thoroughly exhausted.

As the session concluded and Arya removed her gloves, wiped the sweat from her face and looked intently at Philip. She uttered the name, "Garu."

In the excitement and adrenaline of training, he'd failed to see that Arya wasn't just training, she was preparing for a fight. Philip hesitated before responding but made his true feelings known. "I have no interest in watching you get killed."

"I know in my heart that I have to do something about Garu," she said. "I won't let him hurt anyone else… Maybe I can do it with boxing… and you could help me."

"What are you talking about?"

"Let's find a way to beat him with boxing."

Philip shook his head, dismissing the idea.

"I'm asking you, please, come with me. You wanted to gamble…let's bet against him."

"So you're not planning on fighting?"

"We'll do what you said. Bet on some fights."

"He's not going to like seeing you there."

"I don't care."

The following night, though reluctant, Phillip hailed a taxi and provided the driver with the address of the Balaji Boxing Gym.

From the number of cars parked outside, it was clear that it was a busy night. Inside, they saw almost twice as many spectators as there were last time—the whole place packed with locals and foreigners in upscale clothing, waiting for the first fight to begin. Arya looked across the empty ring to the other side and spotted Garu sitting with his men.

"There he is."

He had a drink in his hand and a bottle of scotch on the table. Sandeep and Nurul stood next to his table, chatting. Philip pointed out the two constables one row back, keeping watch.

"I need you to be careful; this guy has the police in his pocket."

"I just want to place a bet," she said, disappearing through the crowd to get to his table.

"Let me do the talking!" he shouted, following behind her.

As soon as they approached him, Garu looked up from his table with a combined look of surprise and disgust. "I know you."

Before Arya could reply, two Indian men walking through the crowd stopped when they saw her, their eyes bulging and erupted into a flurry of conversation she could not understand. Looking more closely at their faces, she recognized them.

"Shit. Those are the guys I knocked out," she whispered to Philip.

They started shouting at Arya, then turned to Sandeep and Nurul, emphatically saying something about her in rapid Bengali. All eyes were migrated towards Arya.

"You hurt these men?" Garu asked, his voice cracking with bewilderment.

"I hurt them," she said, enunciating the words slowly.

Thrown off guard by her confidence and apparent history with the men in his employ, Garu directed his attention at Philip. "Why are you with this woman?" he asked in an authoritative tone.

"I'm her coach, but here tonight I'm just a betting man."

"So you know boxing?" Garu smiled.

"I used to be a professional fighter in England—and now I train her."

Garu burst into laughter, recalling the last time he'd seen Arya cowering on the ground next to her shattered phone.

"I want to fight in the ring," Arya announced.

"We have other places where whores can work."

Philip wanted to stop Aarya from continuing in her tracks, because this wasn't what they'd agreed on, but Garu's insult made him reconsider.

"Are these dogs yours? I beat them up, and I would do the same to you."

By the looks on their faces, the two men she'd humiliated clearly did not regard her as harmless. Sandeep stepped forward and towered over Arya, trying to intimidate her in response.

"Women don't fight here," Garu said, brushing her off.

"I'll fight whoever killed Bimala," she said. They all fell silent. Garu and Nurul's eyes traveled to Sandeep, and Philip gave Arya a stern look, concerned by the direction she was taking the conversation.

"Sandeep is a real fighter. You are a tourist," Garu said. "Go away."

"I'll bet you $10,000 I'll beat him in a boxing match. Here. In front of everyone."

"What are you doing?" Philip said. "You can't fight him."

"I need you to trust me."

"You say you are a boxer and a gambler. What will you do?" They all looked to Philip to see how he would respond.

"I'll match her bet."

Garu, Nurul, and the two men roared with laughter. Sandeep kept his deadpan stare, insulted by the mere idea of sharing the ring with a woman.

"Prove to me you both have twenty thousand dollars in cash. Otherwise, get the fuck out."

Philip pulled out his phone, logged into his banking app, and showed Garu the screen—a balance of $121,432 in his checking account.

"Okay, come next week, and Sandeep will kill your woman in the ring."

"I need time to train her for this fight," Philip said, putting the phone away. "We need twelve weeks."

"Four weeks, no more."

"There's one more thing," Arya said. "If I win, you let the girl go."

"What girl?" Garu sneered.

"The young one."

Garu looked over at Sandeep, trying to understand how she could know. "If you win, I'll give you any whore you want."

Without saying more, Arya turned to leave, and Philip followed her back through the crowd and out the door of the Balaji Boxing Gym.

"What the fuck did I just let you do?" he said, walking out to the sea of parked cars outside.

"You didn't have to match my bet."

"It's not the money. We don't know what kind of fighter this Sandeep guy is—after what he did to you the other night. How can I let you do this?"

"I know it's going to sound strange, but I know in my gut this is the right thing to do."

"I need a drink," Philip said, rubbing his eyes. "Let's see if I can get you in fighting shape for this. If you're not ready for any reason, I'm pulling you out."

21.

IN THE MORNING, Arya took an autorickshaw to Karuna Dan. She aided Sister Catherine with first-period English and sat close to Gita and Podip in the back of the room, gently encouraging them through their assignments. She found Sister Maria during the first recess and sat with her on one of the outside benches, telling her everything—why she went, the interaction with Garu, the wager, who she was fighting. Sister Maria listened, quietly nodding throughout.

"Perhaps God has chosen you for this," she said, surprising Arya with her openness.

"Philip and I agreed that I can't come here for the next four weeks."

"Does he think you can win?"

"I don't know what he thinks, but he's committed to training me twice a day, every day until the fight."

"Maybe you will be the one to teach Garu a lesson. Philip would not agree to this if he did not believe in you, but Gita and Podip will be upset that you won't be seeing them for a month."

At the end of the school day, when Arya was getting ready to leave, Sister Maria waved the children over from the playground area.

"You have to tell them," Sister Maria whispered.

As Gita and Podip came running up, Arya got on her knees to speak at eye level.

"There's something important I must do, so I won't be able to come for a while."

"Are you leaving Kolkata?" Gita asked at once, perceptive to the transient nature of volunteers.

"No, I'm staying here, but I'll be working, not too far away."

Podip's shoulders slumped forward at the familiar reality.

"What are you working?" Gita asked.

"Do you know what boxing is?" Arya answered, demonstrating a few punches with her fists.

"Arya is an athlete. She plays the sport of boxing," Sister Maria explained.

Arya captured the children's attention, sparking fresh curiosity in their eyes.

"Like fighting?" Podip asked.

"Yes. A warrior like Kali Ma," Sister Maria said, referring to the most famous West Bengal warrior there was.

"Can we go see?" Gita asked, tugging on her sari.

Arya was certain Sister Maria would say no to the request, but she did just the opposite. She agreed to bring Gita and Podip that afternoon to watch her first training session before the fight. They all shared a taxi to the hostel, and Arya led them up to the roof a little earlier than her scheduled time. They found Philip waiting. He showed disapproval in his face the moment he saw them and furiously waved Arya over to speak in private. Sister Maria held onto Gita and Podip, who watched their argument from a distance with keen interest.

"I told you, I'm pulling you out of this fight if you're not committed. No way they can be here. You got to take this seriously."

"I am serious. Don't you think having them here reminds me what this is about?"

"I need you focused."

"The boy just lost his mother; the girl hasn't seen hers in months and probably never will again. Because of Garu. Nothing is going to make me focus more than that."

Philip huffed, eyeing Gita and Podip. "If you want them to be here, you and they are going to have to work for it," he said, marching across the roof to give them orders.

"Go downstairs and bring me small rocks," he said to Podip, outlining with his thumb and index finger something the size of a pebble. "And you," speaking to Gita, "Arya is going to carry you on her shoulders. Go ahead."

Podip looked to Sister Maria for reassurance, so she went with him downstairs to search the courtyard for tiny rocks, while Gita ran toward Arya so that she could lift her up and place her atop her shoulders.

"Don't worry, I'll hold your legs," she said, feeling the girl squirm with excitement standing so tall.

Podip and Sister Maria returned with a small pile of rocks that they placed at the edge of Philip's table, and he signaled for them to stand beside him as he was ready to start the first drill. He positioned Arya several yards away and sat next to Podip at the table with the pebbles between them and started throwing them at Arya, one by one. To avoid being hit, she darted from side to side, using leg strength and core stability with the added weight of Gita on her shoulders. Philip aimed low to avoid hitting the girl, and Podip was happy to throw a few himself. Exhausting the supply, Philip sent him down for two more handfuls.

Sister Maria watched with amusement, though aloof and quiet, thinking about her vision of Kali all those years ago, and how it had heralded a new season in her life. She let the children watch Arya train for forty-five minutes and when the sunlight started to wane, took them home.

The next day, free of obligations, Arya prepared for Philip to push her to her limit, starting with jumping rope in the morning. She went straight into shadowboxing and footwork drills for an hour, followed by a short rest. In the afternoons and evenings, Arya skipped cardio for longer sessions on the pads, working on striking and movement around an opponent.

They continued that schedule for a few days, with Philip insisting that Arya eat well and get plenty of sleep every night. Before the week was through, he also told her that they would be going to the Balaji Boxing Gym during the day to see if they could use the facilities. The roof simply wasn't the right venue to train for a real match.

In the early afternoon, they took a taxi there and met Rakesh on break between classes. He sat on one of the benches outside the locker room, scrolling on his phone. The hall seemed a different place entirely, devoid of all the spectators and the fixtures Garu brought in each fight night. Philip explained the situation, upsetting Rakesh that such a spectacle would be taking place at his gym.

"I didn't know Garu allowed women to fight…" he said, processing the information.

"He's made an exception for us," Philip said. "And we can pay to use your gym…"

"Come in," he said. "We'll figure something out."

Rakesh showed them around the gym, taking them around the heavy bags, then to the weights, jump ropes, and medicine balls at the other side of the space. He offered a nominal day rate.

"I have a class coming later, but you can start today if you wish."

To get accustomed to training, Philip accepted the offer and had Arya change into her gear, which she'd brought in the duffle over her shoulder. She went to the locker room to change, and when she came out, a few of Rakesh's female trainees had come in and were warming up around the gym. They looked to be teenagers, between the ages of fourteen and eighteen.

Philip had Arya warm up on the heavy bags, since it was a luxury not available at the hostel. He gave her combinations to try, changing them every few minutes to keep her mind sharp and make her break a sweat. Afterward, he put her through a grueling session with the pads, using the full size of an Olympic ring to move around, giving her time on the same canvas where she would meet Sandeep.

After a short rest, Arya was back on the heavy bag, hitting it like she'd just walked in. Rakesh and his trainees peered over to look because of the loud cracking sounds that reverberated through the gym.

"Maybe you're not crazy," Rakesh said, watching Arya move.

"We're going to need a sparring partner. Someone tall and strong," Philip replied.

• • •

Garu was confident Arya's wager would translate into easy money. The vainglory of one meddlesome female tourist had no chance in the ring against Sandeep. Over the days that followed, he placed his focus on Yunni, making sure she fell in line so she could be sold to the highest bidder. Foreigners with money and illicit tastes often came to Kolkata to buy young girls. Sitting at his desk at the jewelry store with Sandeep and Nurul, he discussed the logistics of getting his prize ready.

"Tell me about Yunni," he demanded of Sandeep.

"Her body has grown accustomed to brown sugar."

"She does not fall asleep now when we give it to her," Nurul added. "She is eager for us to come back now. I believe she is ready."

"Good. Tell Dhriti to dress her and start showing her to the customers. Let's see what price she is worth."

"Yessir," Nurul said, standing up to leave, Sandeep getting up to join him.

"Not you, Sandeep. I must speak with you," Garu said, motioning for Nurul to leave them alone.

When the door closed behind him, Garu lit a cigarette and studied the rugged face of his top enforcer, sensing something different about him. Born in a remote rural village in Orissa, several hours away by train, Sandeep hadn't seen plumbing or air-conditioning until he arrived in Kolkata and fell into Garu's folds as a teenage boy. Since then, he'd obeyed every command, fulfilling every request without question. Garu allowed him to exchange brutality for comfort, and for that, he'd been loyally grateful, but now, he sensed dissent.

"I hear from Arjan you are not training."

"Training?" Sandeep asked, a hint of disgust in his voice. "You expect me to train for this fight? I am humiliated."

"I expect you to protect my money."

"And your spectators… You are not embarrassed to put on this charade?"

"They want a fight; they will see a fight. I do not care what anyone thinks. This is my house. Something was delivered to me. Look at this," he said, sliding a piece of paper across the desk. It was an account statement belonging to Philip Tyers from the Bank of England, confirming that the account he'd shown them on his phone was real.

"What is this?" Sandeep said, attempting to translate a sum of British pounds into Indian rupees in his head.

"This is from the British man. He would not put her in the ring if she could not fight. You heard how she hurt the others. Go train!" Garu shouted.

Sandeep left the jewelry store filled with anger. He looked away from his trailing reflection in the retail store windows as he walked down the street on the way to his boxing gym. It was a private facility that Garu paid for, with a discrete entrance a few steps down from the sidewalk. Inside, the walls were mirrored, further aggravating Sandeep because he could not stand to look at himself.

"You're late," his trainer Arjan said, a middle-aged boxing coach with a crooked nose from too many punches.

Sandeep ignored the comment and got changed. He went through the motions until halfway through the heavy bag workout—he stopped and took off his training gloves.

"That's enough for today…" he said, reaching for his water.

"Your fight is in three weeks," Arjan said. "We're not done."

"I'm fighting a whore," he said, sauntering towards the locker room. "I don't need to train."

"We're not finished," Arjan shouted at his back.

Sandeep turned around and walked over to Arjan, staring him down. He punched the mirror behind him, inches from his head, cracking it with his wrapped fist.

"When Garu asks, tell him I am training," he said, before walking out.

22.

BY THE SECOND week of training, Philip was pleased with Arya's strength and accuracy, so he shifted the focus of the training to improve her conditioning. He wanted her to tire Sandeep in the early rounds. As the lighter, faster boxer, he expected her to have impeccable stamina and maintain constant evasive movement. Only that way could she avoid getting hit by Sandeep's big punches and create a window where she might be able to land her own.

With less resistance from Philip than Arya expected, he allowed Sister Maria to bring Gita and Podip to the hostel to watch another training session. Excited by the idea of having a real warrior in their lives, they were very eager to come and filled Sister Maria's ears with talk of the matter. They arrived on Sudder Street that afternoon, with a bit of winter chill in the October air, and found Arya and Philip standing outside the entrance.

They looked and saw that Philip had commissioned a pulled rickshaw—not one of the motorized ones—and it and the driver were positioned in front of the hostel, awaiting his plans. Kolkata remained as one of the last cities in India that still allowed the hand pulled rickshaws, viewed around the world as a dehumanizing remnant of British colonial times. It was a cart on wheels with long handles, allowing a person to carry passengers on the back for a fare. Hostel guests coming and going stopped to stare at what was happening, standing beside curious Babu and Chaiwallah.

"Alright. Here's what's going to happen," Philip started. "You two are going to ride in the back, and Arya is going to run with you down the street and back. Okay?"

Gita and Podip giggled at the notion of being included again. The driver stood next to his rickshaw, the sole means of his prosperity, waiting with everyone else to learn the reason he'd been stopped. For a man in his sixties, with a long gray beard, his body was lean from decades of running through the streets. Philip picked Gita and Podip up and placed them in the carriage.

"Arya, stand in the front and hold the handles," he said, handing the driver more than sufficient payment for use of his conveyance.

He took the money and stood with a perplexed look as Arya grabbed the handles and lifted them off the ground. A few of the passing pedestrians stopped to watch the peculiar sight, gathering amongst the hostel guests and staff outside. Sister Maria stood with Jun and Hiro, clenching her fists in anticipation.

"Take them to the end of the street and back as fast as you can," Philip instructed. "Go!"

Arya took off running down the street, with Gita and Podip laughing wildly in back. She took a wide turn at the intersection and came back. More pedestrians had gathered to observe the spectacle.

"That's much harder than it looks," Arya said, breathing hard in front of the hostel.

"I need you running circles around this guy. Push yourself as hard as you can. Go!" he screamed, sending her off again.

She ran faster to the end and back, working her muscles and lungs at maximum effort. When she returned, a man stepped out of the crowd and began cursing in Bengali and spitting on the ground to show disrespect.

"What's with him?"

"There is a caste system here," Sister Maria replied. "He does not like seeing you with…people of a lower caste." She directed her gaze at the rickshaw driver, then Gita and Podip.

"Doesn't matter," Philip interrupted. "Ain't everyone gonna cheer for you in a boxing match. Go!"

Arya ran again, as fast as she could, to the intersection, with the rickshaw bouncing on the uneven pavement behind her several more times, the children laughing all the while. After several more rounds, her arms and legs were exhausted; her clothes soaked with sweat. That evening, Gita and Podip returned home too ecstatic to fall asleep at their usual bedtime, envisioning the battle that awaited.

Each day, Philip pushed Arya, driving as much incremental improvement in her technique and conditioning in the short amount of time they had. She was a far cry from the fighter he'd trained that first day, but the changes were hardly the reassurance he needed for her to get into the ring against a larger, stronger man.

At the Balaji Boxing Gym, Philip ran Arya through conditioning drills on the heavy bags, three-minutes on, one-minute off. Rakesh's female students were in awe. Arya was a boxer like them, yet quite foreign and intriguing. In private, Philip had a conversation with Rakesh, in which he inquired about Sandeep and his boxing record.

According to Rakesh, Sandeep was a devastating opponent, and it was completely ludicrous that he be allowed to fight a woman. "He is a man raised on hate, who boxes with no class."

The words haunted Philip each day that he trained Arya, echoing in his mind. But he did not bring up his concerns with her. By the third week, Philip began sparring with Arya himself, desperate to find some assurance that he was not sending her to die.

Wearing gloves and headgear on loan from Rakesh, he boxed with her across the rooftop, trading hard shots—not holding back. His table was clear of the usual bottles, and his mind focused on giving Arya the best chance of surviving against Sandeep. Philip feinted and attacked Arya from troubling angles, using his reach to show her what it's like getting hammered by a significantly taller opponent.

Arya landed two well-timed body shots, working hard to get on the inside, but when she went in for a third, Philip cracked Arya with a hard left hook, spinning her head around. She wobbled but kept standing and shook it off, coming at him again. Without a second's pause, he clobbered her over the head with an easy overhand right, putting her down on the cement floor. She spit out her bloody mouthguard and looked up in disbelief.

"What was that?"

"You have to make me miss!" he shouted back at her. "That's the way to win. Make me miss and counter. Get me tired. Focus!"

"I wasn't expecting that," she said, picking herself up off the floor.

"That's the point!" he screamed. "You'll get killed in the ring. You have to expect everything. Have an answer to every punch, God damn it!" Philip yanked off his gloves and headgear, tossing them aside in frustration. He went to the edge of the roof and took a moment to himself, facing away from her.

"What's wrong with you?"

He took several deep breaths, trying to keep calm. "The guy you're fighting...Sandeep. He's never lost before. He's filled with hate, and he's going to hurt you…bad."

"You're saying I can't win?"

"Do you think you can?" he answered back at her, continuing to look out over the city.

Arya wrestled her gloves and headgear off and yanked Philip's shoulder around to continue the conversation face-to-face. "If you don't believe I can win, that's fine. What do you believe?"

"I believe good people can die stupid deaths," he replied, with a flat tone of voice, trying to speak as earnestly as possible.

"You believe you're meant to live out the rest of your miserable days here. Drunk and alone. And you also know that's a pile of bullshit."

"They were killed!" Philip screamed at her.

Arya's demeanor changed and her shoulders fell. "What?"

"My family…because of decisions I made in the ring. I wouldn't throw the fight…so they killed them, my wife and son."

"Philip, I'm so sorry…"

"I don't want anyone else to die because of me," he said, wiping tears from his eyes. "You can't do this."

Arya placed her hand on Philip's shoulder and looked into his eyes. "I believe we met for a reason. Neither of us really belongs here. All I set out to do was get clean, but here we are. If I get hurt in that ring, it isn't your fault."

"That's not true," he said, with great pain in his eyes.

"I'm fighting for everything I ever believed in with this. I see Sister Maria and the others giving everything they've got to serving others, and this is my chance to do something that makes a difference. It doesn't matter if you think I don't have a chance in there because I know this is what I was meant to do."

23.

WITH ONLY A week left before the fight, Arya and Philip went to the gym for their daily training session and found that Rakesh had finally brought a sparring partner for Arya. At nineteen and a champion in her league, she stood almost half a foot taller than Arya. Even though no sparring session could prepare her for Sandeep, Philip was glad to add variety and a new challenge to Arya's training.

After a short warm-up, Arya climbed into the ring with the young woman. Rakesh rang the bell, and the other girl came out aggressively, using her height advantage, leading with her long jab. She had impressive stamina, firing a high volume of shots, making Arya tired from all the evasive maneuvering.

"She's perfect," Philip said, watching the exchange.

"I knew you would be happy," Rakesh smiled.

To avoid getting directly in the line of fire, Arya worked her angles on her counters, ducking and slipping, using every opportunity to throw a counter punch. Some of the girls from Rakesh's younger class came close to watch.

"Arya has talent. This girl is the champion in her league," Rakesh said, giving them a one-minute break.

"She'll need more than that."

"Garu's money keeps this gym open, but I would spit on him if I could. Everyone here hopes your woman is the winner."

They sparred for a total of six rounds, boxing respectfully, refraining from throwing haymakers or knockout punches.

Later that night, Philip made Arya spar with him one more time, warning that he would not hold back and inviting her to do the same. They moved around the rooftop, trading shots, breathing heavily. At first, Philip dominated her with his size and aggressive style, but slowly, Arya used her speed to gain the upper hand.

She cracked Philip on the chin with a hard left hook, and his counter flew overhead, missing wildly. She followed her attack with an uppercut, stunning him, and then delivered a hard right hand that knocked Philip off his feet. He tumbled and crashed onto the cement floor.

He lay there a few seconds, taking deep breaths, then began fidgeting with his gloves and headgear to get them off. "I've never been so happy to get punched in the face," he said, spitting out his mouthguard and looking up at Arya in a daze.

A few days later, Sister Maria brought Gita and Podip to the hostel to see Arya again. Philip had managed to find the same rickshaw driver, so when they arrived, the carriage was already waiting for them on the street outside the front door. Philip lifted Gita and Podip into the carriage, and invited Sister Maria to get in beside them, adding more weight for Arya to pull.

The rickshaw driver joined the crowd that had gathered. Arya stepped in between the handles, lifted them off the ground, and started sprinting as fast as she could. She ran to the intersection and back several times as Gita and Podip howled with joy, Sister Maria laughing beside them. She stopped in front of the hostel to rest for a minute, winded from the activity.

Out of the mixed crowd of curious pedestrians and amused hostel guests, a small group of men seemed less pleased than the others and began hurling insults at Arya, directing some at the rickshaw driver as well for his involvement in the spectacle. To spite them, Arya chauffeured the driver in his own carriage, running to the end of the street and back again as Gita and Podip cheered from in front of the hostel.

"Kali fight!" Gita suddenly cried out.

Podip joined in. "Kali fight!" he emphasized loudly.

Feeding off each other, they were soon screaming "Kali fight!" over and over, while Arya did her laps up and down the street. It was a young man in the crowd, a local, who first joined in with Gita and Podip.

"Kali fight! Kali fight! Kali fight!" they chanted and soon others joined in, too.

As Arya rounded the bend in front of the hostel for the last time, Chaiwallah, Jun, Hiro, Philip, Sister Maria, Gita, Podip, and over a dozen other people were cheering for her. "Kali fight! Kali fight! Kali fight!"

With the children so happy, Sister Maria agreed to take them to see Arya train one last time at the gym two days before the match. Philip and Arya were doing pad work in the ring when they arrived, and they stood with Rakesh and his trainees, admiring the display. Arya hit her combinations well, moving her head side to side, using footwork and finesse.

"Kali fight! Kali fight! Kali fight!" Gita and Podip would not stop cheering—to the amusement of Rakesh and his trainees.

Returning to the hostel, Philip gave Arya specific instructions to let her body rest, eat well, and avoid strenuous activity for the next twenty-four hours before the fight. She took Philip's advice, spending the better part of her time in her room, envisioning the fight. In the evening, a few hours before bedtime, she had an unexpected knock at the door.

She opened it and saw Sister Maria standing there, holding a package under her arm. She handed it to Arya and then stepped in and took a seat at the edge of the bed. Arya peeled back the wrapping paper. In her hands, she held a black sports jersey with the silhouette of the goddess Kali printed on the front in red.

"They're calling you by her name; you might as well wear it."

"Thank you, Sister. I don't know what to say—"

"Kali fight," she said, pumping her fist in the air. "May God protect and watch over you, and let your victory be a testament to his glory."

24.

ON THE MORNING of Arya's fight, Philip had two errands. The first was a trip to the bank so that he could withdraw the cash needed for the wager. The second errand was personal, which he didn't tell anyone about. He wanted to see the brothel for himself, this place that created Gita and Podip, where women like Bimala were treated ruthlessly. It represented everything that Arya wished to fight against, and he needed to see it.

He hailed a taxi on Sudder Street, heading for Bhowanipore. Memories of the day preceding his last bout years ago flooded his mind; how conflicted he'd been after his meeting at the bar with Paulie. Watching the city from his window, Philip had the reminiscent sensation, the feeling of once again permitting a match that had the potential to ruin lives. The taxi came to a halt not far from the school, where Arya would have been volunteering that day.

He instructed the taxi driver to wait and approached the brothel's entrance. At this hour, there was no foot traffic in or out, yet merely laying eyes on the place made it more real. Philip suddenly understood that Garu and Paulie were two of a kind. A surge of determination welled up in Philip, amplifying his outlandish hope for Arya's victory.

Just then, a young woman emerged from the doorway and stopped in front of Philip. She was Dhriti, hardly more than a girl in his eyes.

"Friend of Kali fight?" she asked in a hushed tone.

"I am," he said, surprised to hear the name far from Sudder Street.

Dhriti quickly looked both ways, then reached into her sari. She handed Philip something—it was a cell phone, turned off, with a big crack on its screen.

"Why are you giving this to me? It's broken—"

"Please—" she replied, imploring him with her eyes to take the phone. She held his gaze for a lingering moment before heading inside. Still perplexed, Philip pocketed the phone and climbed back into the taxi.

The closest international bank presented a sharp contrast to his prior location—a gleaming red and white establishment on Chowringhee Lane. Philip entered through the automatic glass doors and stood in the immaculate reception area. After a short wait, he was ushered into a clear glass office. Inside sat a well-groomed, rotund bank manager, his name tag reading "Suraj." Behind him, a poster showcased an Indian family dressed in Western attire, enjoying a picnic in a park. The words "Families First" overlay the image.

Suraj glanced over the withdrawal form Philip had filled out.

"We will provide you with a check—"

"Cash, please."

Suraj raised an eyebrow at the request for such a substantial amount in cash. Several minutes later, Philip left the bank with forty lakhs discreetly tucked inside an inner pocket of his lightweight jacket.

He made his way back to the hostel, heading directly to Arya's room. Inside, he discovered her engrossed in organizing her finances as well, money arranged in stacks on the bed.

"I'm committed to this," Arya declared, looking up at him. All the money and resources she possessed laid bare.

"Me too."

25.

AT SEVEN IN the evening, they met Sister Maria in the courtyard and took a taxi to the Balaji Boxing Gym. The bouncers laughed at the sight of Sister Maria in her nun's sari at an illegal betting venue. But she entered with two people who did look the part, so they let her in.

The gym where she'd had just taken Gita and Podip to see Arya practice had been transformed into a bustling fight venue, brimming with eager spectators. Rows of folding metal chairs surrounded the ring, and bright lights beamed down from overhead. At two separate tables, bartenders handed out beer and a selection of liquor from coolers on display.

Philip guided Arya and Sister Maria directly through the throng of spectators to the women's locker room and went in alongside them. They settled on a long wooden bench that split the room. As Philip wrapped Arya's hands, Sister Maria sat close, her lips moving in silent prayer. *Please, God, let her win. Make her fierce like Kali, like you did for me once.*

Once he was done, Arya rose and removed her hoodie, unveiling the tank top beneath it with the image of Kali.

"Nice shirt," Philip said, slipping her gloves on.

Arya rolled her shoulders, loosening them up as she had done before so many fights. None had ever carried the weight of this one, and she realized that for the first time, her fists and heart were aligned. She wasn't just fighting for a way to stay in Kolkata, but for her own dignity as well.

Philip guided her through a gentle session of shadowboxing, ensuring she was warmed up and limber. In the absence of conversation, Philip thought about his last match, and the awful events that ensued. He could not help picturing Arya lying on the canvas the way he'd once found Anna and Dorian on the kitchen floor.

After a short while, Rakesh entered the locker room, signaling that it was time.

Emerging onto the floor, they made their way to Arya's designated corner. Arya and Philip then ascended into the ring, leaving Sister Maria positioned just beyond the ropes. From their vantage point, they spotted Garu seated two rows back from ringside, surrounded by his crew. Directly behind them, two alert police constables stood watch. It seemed so undeserved for someone like that to have men in uniform guarding him.

Emerging from the men's locker room, Sandeep and his trainer, Arjan, headed to the opposite corner and climbed into the ring. Arya tracked him with her eyes, thinking about the women and children he'd hurt. Some in the crowd cheered, recognizing Sandeep from his previous fights. But a wave of unease spread as spectators noticed the stark contrast between the young woman and the much larger male opponent about to face off.

A man in a navy blazer and white Indian kurta stepped forward with a wireless microphone. His voice echoed throughout the gym, calling Arya and Sandeep to the ring's center. The size difference between them terrified Sister Maria, who clutched the edges of her sari and continued to pray.

"This is the bout between Arya and Sandeep. Ten rounds," the announcer proclaimed. "Place your bets now," he added, gesturing towards Garu's treasurer, seated nearby, right next to the constables.

While some in the audience chuckled at the apparent mismatch, deeming the outcome a foregone conclusion, a few ventured over to place bets. Garu, confident and grinning, was already envisioning the hefty payout he'd pocket by night's end.

After a brief ten minutes of frenzied betting, a referee took center stage in the ring and instructed Arya and Sandeep to touch gloves before directing them back to their respective corners.

"Alright. Here we go. Stay sharp," Philip said, rubbing Arya's shoulders for a second before ducking down behind the ropes. "This is what we came for!"

The bell rang, signaling the start of round one.

Both fighters charged from their corners. Sandeep, clearly towering over Arya, threw a jab that missed as it whisked over her shoulder. Quickly adapting, she evaded his next attempt and retaliated with a sharp left hook, landing squarely on Sandeep's cheekbone, jerking his head to the side. The crowd's energy shifted palpably, as spectators leaned forward in their seats, surprised and invigorated by the smaller fighter's powerful hit in just the opening moments.

Sandeep halted, a raw sting of humiliation searing through him. Gritting his teeth, he surged at Arya, thrusting aggressively with his left. She threw quick jabs to his midsection, but they didn't seem to hurt at all. He retaliated with fierce right hooks aimed at her shoulders and ribs, forcing her to dance back, reeling from the force. Hungry for a knockout, he swung his right even higher, but Arya was quick. She ducked and fired back a hard left, rocking his head sideways again.

"That's it!" Philip shouted from the corner.

"She's making him angry!" Sister Maria exclaimed, nervously clenching her fists.

To make use of his size advantage, Sandeep leaned on Arya, using his weight to apply downward pressure and smother her strikes. Before the referee could break them apart, he clobbered her over the head with his right hand. Fighting to get free from underneath, she stepped back and caught a snapping jab that opened a cut under her eye as she stumbled back against the ropes.

Sensing his chance to finish the fight early, Sandeep charged forward, aiming for that knockout punch. Arya held her ground, raising her defenses against a storm of blows aimed squarely at her head. But one fierce straight right found its mark, whipping her head back.

She lost her footing and fell onto the canvas while Sandeep stepped back, throwing a glance over at Garu's table.

"No!" Sister Maria exclaimed, gripping Philip's arm tightly.

"Get up, Arya!" Philip shouted. "Only twenty-five seconds left!"

The referee began his count, and with determination, Arya started pushing herself off the canvas to her knees.

"Four...five...six...seven..."

Arya rose to her feet, a thin stream of blood dripping from her nose. The referee gestured for her to raise her gloves, examining her eyes closely to gauge her ability to proceed. After a tense pause, he signaled for the fight to continue. A wave of excitement pulsed through the spectators, setting off a flurry of chatter throughout the gym.

Sandeep lunged forward, hounding her around the ring, throwing punches with raw aggression, but most went astray. Arya ducked and weaved, dodging his onslaught for the remainder of the round until the clang of three bells called them back to their corners.

Philip swiftly tossed a stool through the ropes and climbed in. He removed her mouthguard and wiped the blood from her face before rubbing ointment on her cheekbones and cut, so that she could take the punches better. Arya's chest rapidly rose as she tried to regain her breath before the next round.

"Okay. You got through round one. You've said your introductions. Now the fight starts. Are you ready?"

"He hits hard."

"But you're fast. Increase the volume. More punches. Make him move. Make him chase you. You got this. Let's go!"

It felt as though only a moment had passed, yet the bell signaled the start of the next round. Arya stood up from her stool and faced Sandeep in the center of the ring again. She threw out short punches to keep him at a distance, but they just bounced off his gloves without impact. To prevent Sandeep from pinning her against the ropes again, she moved away quickly. He marched after her, taking big steps in an effort to close the gap.

He punched her arms and sides in wide arcs, throwing off her balance. As she rose her hands to cover her face, Sandeep attacked her midsection, cracking her ribs and stealing her breath away. As she bent over from the force of the hit, he struck her temple with a right hook that took her down again. She grabbed onto the ropes and pulled herself up before the ref's count even began.

"She's tough!" Sister Maria said to Philip, her grip tightening on the edge of the platform.

"Stay away!" Philip shouted, seeing Sandeep queuing up a big attack.

Arya attempted to stay away, but Sandeep continued to pressure her, making her answer his punches. She jabbed out repeatedly to block him from getting too close, yet the blows did not seem to faze him. A left hook caught her off guard and sent her fleeing towards the ropes. Sandeep took the opportunity and pummeled her with body shots. Arya covered up and cowered, too stunned to fight back or even move, desperately hoping not to be knocked out.

"Volume! Now!" Philip yelled from across the ring.

Arya threw punch after punch at Sandeep as she tried to escape him. He trudged after her, his feet pounding the canvas. As her energy began to wane, Arya heard the sound of three bells, indicating that the round was over. Relieved, she dropped her arms to her sides and walked away from Sandeep as he muttered curses at her back.

"How we doing?" Philip asked, pulling out the stool for Arya.

She crashed down hard on it, breathing heavily.

"He's winning… I can't get to him…"

"You're still in it! He thought he'd have you by now. He doesn't think he's winning, and he's desperate to knock you out. Let him try. Make him miss and then crack him as hard as you can. When he's weak, hit him with volume. He's not as tough as you think he is. You can do this!"

26.

THE AUDIENCE SHIFTED in their seats as the bell sounded for the third round, and the air was thick with anticipation. Arya and Sandeep squared off, fists raised, prepared to fight. She lowered her guard and stepped forward, daring Sandeep to hit her. As he threw a right hand, Arya ducked, then delivered a powerful left hook that hit the side of his face.

A flash of red.

A deep cut appeared beneath Sandeep's right eye, making Garu show the worry on his face.

"Yes!" Philip screamed from the corner. "Keep going!"

Sandeep stared in shock at the blood on his glove from his face. His gaze quickly shifted to Garu, and then Arya was upon him. She moved swiftly, punching with lightning jabs, outboxing him with quick strikes.

Sandeep straightened his arm and pushed his glove in her face to blind her. He then threw a powerful right hook that landed on the side of her head, making her stumble back. He stepped forward, pushing against her, preventing any counterattacks as he hit her sides with relentless force. Arya's guard came down, and he delivered another solid punch in the form of a stiff jab, throwing her into the corner. She used the ropes to keep herself upright, struggling to stay on her feet.

"Get off the ropes! Get out of the corner!" Philip shouted.

She braced herself against Sandeep's assault, bearing the brunt of it with her arms in front of her face.

Three bells signaled the end of the round.

Sandeep glanced at Garu, who bore an offended expression on his face, vigorously shaking his head in disapproval.

Arya sat in the corner, ribs aching and blood dripping from her nose. Her right eye was swelling and she could barely hear Philip's voice as he spoke quickly. But two words drowned out the sounds of her loud heartbeat and ragged breathing.

"Arya, look."

She twisted her head to see what he was pointing to behind her. Sister Maria stood outside the ropes near them, her hands clasped together in appreciation of the sight as well.

About a dozen teenage girls from the Balaji Gym who had previously watched Arya train eagerly gathered at the entrance. Their excitement was palpable as they attempted to push their way into the gym, but the bouncers held firm, denying them access. Undeterred, some stayed near the door, hoping to catch fleeting moments of the inside action, while others drifted towards dust-coated windows, searching for a clearer view.

Philip turned to Arya with an inspired grin. "They're here for you."

The words gave her strength. She thought of Gita and Podip, and it filled her with a sense of urgency to win.

The bell signaled the start of round four. Emerging from his corner, Sandeep adopted a more guarded stance for the first time, hands poised defensively. Moving with traditional boxing techniques, he pressed forward, launching precise one-two combinations, appearing like a transformed fighter. Arya, taken aback by his sudden shift in tactics, was caught unprepared for a swift uppercut that connected with her chin, snapping her head backwards. Capitalizing on the moment, Sandeep delivered a sharp right, sending a spray of blood and sweat from Arya's face as she tumbled dramatically to the canvas.

"Philip! She's hurt!" Sister Maria cried out.

The referee started the count, pushing Sandeep out of the way.

"One… two… three…"

Philip clenched the edge of the platform, his gaze locked onto Arya, searching for signs of her resilience. As Arya stirred, a faint glimmer of movement, he found himself holding his breath.

"…five...six...seven...eight…"

Arya struggled to stand, staggering and unsteady on her feet. The referee held her gloves and looked into her eyes to see if she could continue the fight. He let go, and Sandeep wasted no time in rushing her, quickly pushing her back into the ropes. He delivered a left hook and wound up his right hand for the finishing blow.

"She can't go on!" Sister Maria exclaimed, questioning whether Philip should intervene and halt the fight.

"Make him miss!" Philip shouted.

Arya deftly ducked beneath Sandeep's swinging fist, then retaliated with a sharp right hand, exacerbating the cut beneath his eye, drawing more blood.

"Stay off the ropes! Keep him moving!"

Following Philip's advice, Arya moved to the center of the ring, tired but determined. Sandeep kept coming, but she could hear his breathing getting heavier. Recognizing his fatigue, Arya made him chase her, throwing punches and then moving back quickly. She tired herself out too, but held on.

The bell rang, ending the round, and Arya had managed to avoid getting knocked down again.

She collapsed onto her stool in the corner, breathing heavily, exhausted, and bloodied.

"I'm sorry—" she started. "I can't do it."

"Don't do that," Philip said, lifting her chin up.

"I can't beat him." She clenched her teeth to fight back the tears.

"You can beat him. You're one punch away from doing it. Think about why you're here—what all this means to you."

She looked around the room, the foreignness of where she was, suddenly aware how far she'd come in a short time.

"What you've overcome... That takes strength. And getting in the ring with him takes courage, a special kind of courage. Sister Maria believes in you. Those kids believe in you. I believe in you. I haven't believed in anything in a long time. But I see you fight, and it's like a wake-up call. Haven't had much to believe in lately, but watching you... It reminds me I have more to do in this life. But you're fighting for those who can't right now. So you get back in there, you knock him down. Do it for them, for you, do it for a shot at something better. I know what you're made of. Show them." He gestured at the crowd. Her heart raced as adrenaline coursed through her veins. She cast a glance over her shoulder at Sister Maria and saw a fleeting expression of tranquility.

The bell rang for round five.

Sandeep stepped out of his corner ready to regain his dignity. He came at Arya with a long jab, but she slid aside, dodging the punch. A retaliating left hook smashed into the side of his face, followed by another right hook that made his head spin. Before he knew what happened, she dropped levels and hammered him in the body with powerful liver punches—forcing him back into the ropes as the crowd roared in delight. Some spectators jumped up from their seats, egged on by the unexpected turnaround.

"Light him up! Light him up!" Philip screamed.

Sandeep fought back at Arya with all his might, on the brink of being knocked out for the first time in the match. At the entrance of Balaji Boxing Gym, more young female trainees from Rakesh's classes had gathered in front of the bouncers, trying to get a peek inside. From where Sister Maria and Philip were standing outside, they could hear them chanting, "Kali fight!"

Sandeep desperately tried to regain control over Arya by leaning on her and pressing down on her neck with his arm. He attempted to connect with an uppercut holding her there, but Arya kept her guard up, wrapping her arms around him to avoid getting knocked out.

The referee came to separate them, with a warning to Sandeep on holding, and let the fight resume.

From the doorway of the gym, the chants swelled, echoing louder and more insistent, "Kali fight! Kali fight! Kali fight!" The rhythmic call reached Garu's ears, as well as those of the spectators seated nearest to the entrance. One by one, like a spark igniting a flame, they picked up the chant. It spread swiftly through the crowd, each voice joining the growing chorus.

"Stay on him! Make him miss!" Philip instructed from her corner.

"What a disgrace! Get her!" Garu yelled, spouting out a tirade of obscenities in Bengali. "And tell them to shut up," he barked at Nurul, and then turned around to the two police officers and offered them a taste of his contempt as well. "Your ugly faces are bad luck for me."

Sandeep came at Arya again, swinging wildly, looking to end the fight. Arya slipped and fired a right hand that rattled Sandeep's jaw, sending a ripple through his face, and he fell like a rock, pounding the canvas.

The referee started his count.

"One…two…three…four…"

Sandeep, facedown on the canvas, was barely moving.

"five… six… seven… eight…"

"That's it! He's not getting up!" Philip screamed to Sister Maria, grabbing her by the shoulders.

"She won?" Sister Maria said, shocked by the sudden victory.

The people in the audience shouted and whistled, sharing in Arya's victory. Many stood up to applaud, filling the arena with cheers. The referee stopped the count and raised Arya's glove in victory, and she stood, feeling the pride of her accomplishment.

While Arjan hoisted his defeated fighter up and led him to the corner, the bouncers gave up, and Rakesh's students flooded into the building and gathered around Arya's corner. Philip and Sister Maria assisted Arya down through the ropes, and the young women instantly formed a protective circle around her, their voices rising in a united chant: "Kali fight! Kali fight! Kali fight!"

The announcer took his microphone again.

"We have a winner by knockout… Miss Kali Fight!"

Drawn into the fervor, several spectators continued echoing the chant. The words, like a contagious rhythm, reverberated throughout the gym so that every corner of the space pulsed with a collective chant: "Kali fight! Kali fight! Kali fight!"

In the quiet of the locker room, Philip guided Arya to the bench at the center of the room, with Sister Maria close by. Settling her down, he gently removed her gloves and wraps and tenderly cleaned the blood from her face. Slipping back into her streetwear, Arya pulled a sweatshirt over her tank top.

"You did something incredible here tonight, and I'm so damn proud of you. I'm going to make sure we get what he owes us."

Leaving Arya and Sister Maria alone in the locker room, Philip made his way to Garu. As he navigated the throng of spectators, some showered him with accolades for Arya's victory. Unfazed, Philip briskly approached Garu's table where he sat, an empty glass clutched in his hand, seething with words about Sandeep. Behind him, at another table, the bookkeeper was engrossed, meticulously calculating the payouts from bets placed on the boxing match. Far more spectators had wagered on Arya than he'd anticipated. The mounting payout, especially when accounting for Garu's debt to Arya and Philip, was turning out to be a hefty sum.

"She's a cheating whore!" Garu yelled, seeing Philip approaching. "I will not pay."

"It's time to settle. Your man lost," he replied, keeping his voice calm.

"What can you do?" Garu said, squinting at Philip. "This is my house!"

The bookie watched carefully from his table, to see what Garu would say, with the money in the sealed briefcase beside him. At the established four-to-one odds, Garu owed Philip and Arya nearly 28 Lakhs, the equivalent of forty-five thousand American dollars each.

"And you're going to let that girl go," Philip said.

Garu forced an ugly laugh.

"I owe you nothing. Get out!" he shouted, rising to his feet. He anticipated Nurul and his crew would escort Philip out if he dared to argue.

Spotting activity around the briefcase filled with money they were tasked to protect, the constables in the background promptly moved in to assess the situation.

Philip swiftly reached into his pocket, producing a cell phone with a dented frame and cracked screen. He played a video and pivoted the device for Garu to see. The clip displayed Garu violently striking Arya, succeeded by distressing audio capturing the sounds of the assault. As that footage concluded, Philip quickly shifted to the next video. This clip was filmed within the brothel, showing a petite twelve-year-old Yunni, grotesquely dolled up to be sold, laying on the bed in a chilling heroin-induced daze. The secret footage was added by Dhriti to document something that had become too objectionable to allow to continue.

"What is this?" Garu said.

"Leverage. This is our way to make sure everyone finds out about who you are and make sure you pay us what you owe us," Philip said, speaking clearly, standing firm.

The constables and the bookkeeper leaned in, observing Garu's expression of dismay at losing so much money. The taller officer, standing just behind Garu, approached cautiously and gently gave him a tap on the shoulder.

"If a video like this goes public, our hands are tied," he whispered and quickly backed away.

Fuming, Garu slammed his hand on the table, his gaze landing on the bookkeeper, who stood in tense anticipation of the ultimate decision. "Settle it," Garu grumbled.

The bookkeeper quickly consulted his ledger, then unlatched the briefcase. He meticulously counted and handed over the winnings to Philip—two substantial stacks of notes. Without missing a beat, Philip slid them into his jacket pocket.

"Let the girl go," Philip demanded, shooting Garu an unyielding stare.

Without another word, he made his way back to the locker room, acutely aware of the weight pressing against the inside of his jacket. He was eager to regroup with Arya and Sister Maria and leave the Balaji Boxing Gym as quickly as possible to avoid any unsolicited confrontations. A taxi idled outside, ready to whisk them away to Sudder Street.

As the car moved, each jolt and bump in the road magnified the soreness in Arya's body. The wind from the open windows drowned out most sounds, leaving her unsure if it was conversation between Philip and Sister Maria that she heard, or the drowned-out voices of people on the radio.

Philip brought ice wrapped in a towel to Arya's hostel room. Handing it to her, she pressed it against her face, trying to soothe the swelling under her eyes. He also summoned Chaiwallah, ordering two mango lassis for her and Sister Maria, and a cold beer for himself. Too drained for solid food, Arya savored the creamy lassi, its sweetness replenishing her energy after the grueling bout. They toasted each other and let themselves enjoy the moment.

"You fought hard for that," Philip said, a softness in his voice.

Arya, cradling the icepack against her cheek, managed a tired but genuine smile. "This is the best day of my life."

Hearing those words, tears burst forth from Sister Maria's eyes, who knew better than most the value of sacrifice.

"God has taken all of you—the light and the dark—and made it something wonderful. That is what Kali has meant to me."

Arya's gaze drifted to the drawing of Kali, then to Sister Maria, with deep love and affection for the nun who had offered unconditional love and acceptance from the first meeting. "Thank you, Sister."

"I must get back," Sister Maria said, standing up to finish her lassi, before gently setting the empty glass down on the nightstand. "One day, when Gita and Podip are mature enough, they'll hear the full account of tonight."

She left the room, and a silence settled between Philip and Arya, intensified by the bundles of money between them on the bed.

"I'll count it again," Philip mumbled.

Arya watched him efficiently sift through the notes, counting one stack and then eyeballing the second, holding them side by side. He slid one of the stacks across the sheets to Arya.

"What are you going to do with it?"

She picked up the stack, fingers trembling slightly.

"I have more than I've ever had before," she whispered. "It means I could stay in Kolkata for maybe another year without having to worry about money."

She now had more than she'd taken from Terrance that night. Drawing in a deep breath, Arya let the reality of her triumph envelop her. Her face and ribs ached more than after any fight she'd been in before, but an overwhelming contentment settled, erasing any regret.

Philip stood up and went to the door.

"Get some rest, you've earned it," he assured her, and closed the door behind him.

27.

THE MORNING AFTER the fight, Sister Maria was delighted to find Yunni standing outside the green gate, waiting to be let in. She gave her food and more appropriate attire, taking the woman's sari from her, and giving her a girl's clothes to wear. She did not see Arya that day.

At the hostel, Arya slept in late, and then remained in bed, too sore to move. When she did manage to leave her room, just to fetch Chaiwallah from downstairs, she wore her sunglasses to hide the dark bruising around her eyes. She didn't search for Philip, and he never made it to her room that day.

On the second morning, Arya decided she was well enough to go to school as long as her sunglasses stayed on. She hailed an autorickshaw to take her there, and when she entered the classroom, Gita and Podip bolted from their seats to embrace her. They hugged her around her waist in a show of admiration, because they sensed her triumph meant more than they could know.

Arya took her place beside Gita and Podip near the rear of the classroom, all set to help them with their English homework. They immersed themselves in their assignments, the quiet noise of teamwork filling the air as they filled their notebooks. A few minutes before the recess bell, the door to the classroom creaked open and Sister Maria stepped inside. She noticed Arya there, her presence bringing immense pleasure to Gita and Podip.

During the break, the children played with each other, and Sister Maria invited Arya to sit beside her in the courtyard. In a hushed and earnest tone, Sister Maria told Arya about Yunni. She recounted the harrowing details of how Yunni endured withdrawal, lying in bed, her body drenched in sweat, and trembling as the potent drugs gradually purged themselves from her system. Sister Maria let out a heavy sigh, concern etched across her face.

"It's heartbreaking to see how even the brief time with Garu has taken such a toll on her," she remarked, her voice filled with empathy and worry.

Arya nodded in agreement, her eyes reflecting compassion for Yunni's situation. "Yes," she said softly, "but at least she's not there anymore."

"You must know… She will be okay because of you."

For the rest of the day, Arya couldn't help but reflect on the praise she had received from Sister Maria. Gratitude welled up within her for Yunni's escape, and her own redemption because, as Sister Maria had said, "God uses even our darkness to serve his will."

That evening, as the sun dipped below the horizon, Arya climbed to the rooftop of the hostel, seeking solace in a familiar presence. The weight of the day's revelations hung heavily in the air, and she wished to confide in Philip, to share her thoughts and emotions with her coach, and the one who'd taken a chance on her. However, when she reached the rooftop, her heart sank. Philip was conspicuously absent. The table and chairs that had been a constant fixture, bearing witness to countless conversations and moments of solace, were gone. There were no traces of empty bottles or cigarette butts.

Arya sprinted down the stairs, through the courtyard, and to the reception area to ask Babu where Philip was.

"He left this for you," he said, handing her a sealed envelope.

Arya took the letter back to her room and sat on the edge of her bed to read it.

Dear Arya,

I am returning to England to visit my wife and son. I never had the strength to do this before, but you gave me the courage. Kali Fight.

There is something for you on the roof—tucked away in a corner under a loose block. I believe you can use it to make a difference.

I believe in you.

Philip.

Arya read the note from Philip with a mixture of relief and sadness. She closed her eyes and pictured him there, walking through tall, wet, cemetery grass to reach the headstones. In her mind, she saw him place flowers before them and cry, releasing years of pain.

She made her way back to the rooftop and carefully searched under the loose block in the corner, as Philip had described. There, she discovered a small recess where Philip had placed all his winnings from the fight.

In the early morning hours at school, Arya sought out Sister Maria to share the news about Philip. As she conveyed the message, Sister Maria's eyes lit up, and she gently pressed her hands together in a gesture of gratitude, a sign that her prayers for Philip had been heard and answered. As they both observed Gita and Podip playing with their friends on the playground, Sister Maria offered a thoughtful perspective.

"He left to confront his past, Arya, but he believes in your future."